PREACHER

by
Luther Butler

To Marshall

Luther Butler

SUNSTONE
PRESS

FIRST EDITION

Printed in the United States of America

Library of Congress Cataloging-in-Publication Data

Butler, Luther, 1929-
    Preacher / by Luther Butler. — 1st ed.
        p.   cm.
    ISBN 0-86534-171-0 : $14.95
    I. Title.
PS3552.U82623P74   1992   91-42294
813' .54—dc20   CIP

Published by SUNSTONE PRESS
           Post Office Box 2321
           Santa Fe, NM 87504-2321 / USA

DEDICATED TO
EASTERN NEW MEXICO UNIVERSITY

**MAY YOUR SONS RISE UP AND CALL YOU
BLESSED**

Thanks, Jo and Luke.

CHAPTER ONE

My name is Hank. I was born in a small New Mexico town, Nara Visa, just over the border from Texas. There is not much there except a long winding road coming down into land that will grow enough grass to run a few cows.

Some dryland farmers dust in wheat and milo every year. Nine times out of ten their crops shrivel up and die before they put out heads. Some years, farmers catch the spring rains right and produce enough to sell a little to elevators dotted along the railroad track.

There was not much to do in my town when I grew up before the Vietnam conflict broke out. Dad did not let me come to town very often, unless he brought me into the First Baptist Church, where sometimes we had a preacher. Lots of times the preachers were college students over from Portales.

Eastern New Mexico University has chairs of religion run by three or four different church groups. Since Eastern is a state school, they have to locate all religious schools off campus in private buildings, something about separation of Church and State. Some of you government people will know more about this than I do.

Anyway, Dad put a stop to me driving the old, blue Dodge pickup into town after I spent the night in jail for getting drunk down at the beer hall along the highway. A highway patrolman knew my old man and let me off with a good talking to, before I backed around and ran right into his patrol car.

All it did was knock his front headlight out and dent his grille. I think that crease in his fender was there before I hit him. If it had not been that I had Sadie in there with me, I would'a hit him a good one for the way he called my mother a dog. After all, us ranch people out there, we do not have much but pride. We got plenty of that. It is all that keeps us together most years, when those dry, southwest winds blow across there, blasting everything in sight.

Sadie put her hand on me and said, "Hank, remember you are only in the tenth grade and driving on a learning permit. He will be hard on your daddy if he wants to be."

Sadie was like me, a rodeo rider. She did barrel riding, while I rode the bulls bareback, with only a fiber rope held in one hand. Been on many a mean one. Even young as I was, I was already in the money at the State Fair over at Albuquerque. A man from Eastern's Ag Department came up to see if I would come to Portales and bull ride soon as I got out of high school.

They let Sadie go on home that night with my friend Jim in the other pickup. His gal scooted over real close to let her in on the outside. When they drove off, it gave my heart a twitch, seeing Sadie over there by herself and that couple melted together in that pickup cab like they were one.

By the time the patrolman got through with me, I was a nervous wreck. He put handcuffs on me and drove me in like I was a common criminal. I mean, my daddy ain't rich, you understand, but he does have a spread out south of town that would cover some of those eastern counties. Never mind it is all brush and rocks with a lot of bunch-grass thrown in for the cows to graze on.

I hardly slept that night, it being almost daylight before Dad came and took care of things so I could go on home. "Son, you made me awful ashamed tonight. Guess you won't be needing the pickup for anything but to haul range cubes in for awhile."

I would have protested, but I still had a puke taste in my mouth that almost choked me. That and the taste of beer kept boiling up. "Sadie and I were planning on running over to a little rodeo at Amarillo this weekend."

"Guess your mother can drive you over in her car. I would take you if it wasn't that the cows are calving. You will have to go with her and like it."

"Aw, she complains if I even put my arm around Sadie."

"Another thing I was going to talk to you about. You are getting too involved, young as you are."

This was one time I knew to keep my mouth shut. After all, she had almost let me have it before I got drunk. If I had stayed with her out in the pickup she would have let me go ahead instead of me quitting by just pulling her bra down and sucking on her a little. Craving for beer ruined it all for me. Now I was going have to start all over with her, and the way Mother was, there was not going to be a chance this weekend unless we could crowd together in a loading chute somewhere.

Anyway, it was the middle of my senior year before I got to take the old Dodge off the place again. I still had not gone all the way with Sadie. Even out riding the pastures with her, she did not feel she could let me lay her without her mother or mine catching us.

I kind of had a feeling our fathers would not have cared. Mothers are different. Close as we lived, there was not a chance we were going to lose each other if something happened and she had a baby. Besides, I always kept a package of condoms hidden in my wallet. Old as they were, they might have sprung a leak and caused a short-term baby.

Only way I could have gotten out of marrying her would have been to join the army or something else 'bout as foolish. Only thing I could have thought about more foolish was joining the Marine Corps, like my daddy did in Korea. Reason he limped so much was 'cause he stopped a bullet in his kneecap. Could have lost his whole leg over that one. They flew him back all the way to Bethesda and operated on him or he'd'a been a one-legged man.

First time I got to drive Sadie any place was to Sunday evening church service. She got so righteous after that sermon she would not even let me put my hand down in front of her dress, and she had let me do that more than once before. Even got a little closer to what I wanted to do than that. Would have made it if her mother had not come out to gather eggs out of the barn. Stupid old chickens, laying their eggs in the hay we were lying in, instead of in the chicken house, where they should have been.

7

She did not say much. Just made us dust the hay off our backs before we could come in to dinner. She did not even say anything even though I had already crawled over on Sadie with both of us still dressed. Well, Sadie did have her blouse halfway undone and I had it unzipped, but still we were decent.

It was not until after dinner, Sadie's ma took me outside by myself. "Hank, I think as much of you as I would my own son if we had one. I am trying to raise Sadie up real decent. I know a boy wants to try out new things. You are too young. I want you to promise me you will not touch Sadie until you marry her."

Now Sadie's mother was no slouch herself. Her Levi's fit across her about as tight as Sadie's. Her breasts were better developed than her daughter's, but she was a well-built woman.

I was kind of bashful about the whole thing, but I did get up the courage to ask, "Not even if I use a rubber?"

"Not even if you use a rubber, Hank. It will be better if you wait until both of you are more mature. Anyway, it will not spoil."

We laughed a little bit after that. She took my hand when we walked back to the house. "I was young also, Hank. Sadie's daddy waited even through the war. You going to Eastern?"

"Thought I would. Rodeo team wants Sadie and me. Thought we could at least be together there."

"We talked about it, Hank. Her daddy and I offered to help you two out if you wanted to get married. She wants to meet other people her age before she settles down. You are both young."

We made it on through high school with frustrations every time we were close together. Senior prom was almost more than I could stand, she all dressed up in a blue evening gown with my white corsage, which I pinned on her myself. It took a lot of will power, me pinning through that flimsy material with my fingers reached 'round in the swell of her breast that way.

Some students got to calling me queer, knowing that I had not ever finished anything with Sadie. "Hank, you don't hurry up, one of us is going to do your job for you," Earnest said in P.E. one day. We were out playing touch behind the gym. I hit him before he knew what happened. Earnest and I went back, 'way back, even before first grade, where we rolled round on the Sunday School floor together. He usually beat me. Today, because I was mad, I won.

"Earnest," I said, after the fight was over, "I am sorry. Something came over me there."

"My fault, Hank," he replied still, trying to get up. "Sadie's the kind of girl every boy in school wants, and you have her. Jealous, I guess."

We patched him up so he could finish out the day. Everyone in school knew what had happened, my flying off the handle that way.

It was spring out on New Mexico's high country. When it rains good there is no prettier place than those big grassy savannahs that seem to reach clear over to the mountains and back. Dad and I were pretty busy that last year in high school; we had cows strung clear south to the river. We should have been worth millions, as much land as we had. It seemed that every time we got ahead, something broke us up.

Take that winter. A blizzard blew in when everything looked like it was going good and winter was about over. A New Mexico blizzard is hell. Our country is wide open on the plains, then it runs into some cedar brakes down in the rough country. There was a lot of dry grama, cows had been grazing when it hit. It was before calving time.

Snow came in on us blowing perpendicular. Strange thing trying to drive in a storm when everything turns to snow. Dad and I tried to feed cottonseed cake during that storm. I missed a week of school with my old, blue pickup full of feed trying to pull as many cows through as we could.

They always say, "Time to feed cattle is before a storm." Person who said that never had over a thousand head out on an open pasture with no windbreaks. We finally cut fence and let them drift. Cows drifted to a fence and then bunched up. Some froze, others smothered. We had a job digging live ones out of snowdrifts that covered the fences.

We came out of it better than Sadie's dad did. He got caught same way we did, only he had given up on winter and ran out of cottonseed cake. Had it not been for us working together, we would have lost a lot more. That was the winter it got so bad they brought in loads of hay in cargo planes and dropped it out for us. Only time I ever appreciated the government.

Usually, they were only interested in making us vaccinate or keep us from shipping diseased cattle. That time they helped. It was strange, me driving that old Dodge over flatland and that airplane down low, with bales of hay bouncing down around me. I mean we had hay all over the place. Right where cows needed it was where they bunched down on the leeward side of a few scraggly cedars and rocks.

Once we got them drifting down into rough country, we saved them. Anyway, it was things like that winter that kept Dad from becoming rich. But there was money for college after high school, especially since there was only one child.

Guess that is why Sadie and I were together so much, her being an only child like me. After the storm, she rode with me 'most every evening, gathering up cattle and bringing them back where we could watch them for calving. Most years we saved ninety-eight percent of our calves because we watched them. Only reason we did not have a higher percent of a calf crop was because we usually lost a few first calf heifers and their calves.

"Hank," Sadie asked, "Do you think we will ever marry?"

My ears perked up. She could get pretty heated up once she started talking about marriage. Some people think it is only a boy who tries to make out. Sadie was different. Guess it was only that she was a girl and afraid of getting pregnant and all that made her a little leery. Anyway, she seemed to bring subjects up just to get me all stirred up.

"What do you mean?"

"Lot of boys go with girls for years and then marry someone else."

I could tell she was wanting me to love her some. I pulled the pickup down behind a hill, which was hard to find out on that open mesa, and pulled her over close. If it had not been getting kind of golden hazy out with the sun getting closer to the horizon, I would have taken longer with her than I did. It was long enough to let her know that I loved her, even though it was only a long kiss, one of those kind where two people melt into each other's arms with their bodies entwined.

All kinds of thoughts went through my head before she pulled away and reminded me we had to bring a small herd in from the willow breaks down on the creek.

We lured cattle with our feed. We would drive away, then stop and throw a few handfuls of feed out. Cows heavy with calves would follow us for as long as they could see us and then stop, until we lured them again.

It made Sadie kind of maternal watching those pregnant cows walk up across the pasture that way with their big bellies and udders. You could tell they were going to calve any day.

Now me, watching a bull and cow mating gets me all heated up and ready to take on anything around. With Sadie it was different. It turned her on bad seeing those mother cows getting ready to drop their calves. It brought out her motherly instincts.

Well, while we were sitting waiting for those cows to catch up with us, we took advantage of the time. It got to where we would bring each other to our peak of sexual enjoyment and then break it off for a cooling off spell. I have to say, Sadie was better at breaking than I was. Still, after her mother was so straight-talking with me, I respected her wishes.

Anyway, I remember after that snowstorm, Dad said, "Hank, it seems you have learned enough. I am going to trust you with the pickup again. Thanks for the help. Guess our death count was not more than one percent. Way buzzards were gathering there for awhile, it looked a lot worse than that. You go ahead and drive your pickup to school. Probably Sadie will want to ride with you."

She did. It was real nice picking her up those early spring mornings, when the only warmth we needed was each other, close together. She could warm up without even trying faster than any girl I ever knew.

Not that there had been that many girls. We lived close to each other for New Mexico ranch country, we were five miles apart. We had been babies together. We belonged together.

Only time I had gone out with another girl was when a little girl had moved in from a place west of Santa Fe. She was Spanish. One of those light-skinned ones whose ancestors came from Spain.

All three of us were in the ninth grade that year. I fell for Rosita hook, line and sinker. Something about me always attracted girls. It could not have been my height. I am less than six feet tall. I thought at times it could have been my athletic ability. I played quarterback, shortstop and guard in three different sports plus being all-'round cowboy in high school rodeo for two years straight.

Rosita would let me do things Sadie would not. But she never let me go all the way with her. She was not like Sadie, who knew I was getting too carried away and would stop me. She would let me think she was going to let me finish up with her, and all a sudden she would knock me away and yell she was not that kind of girl. She was not near as much fun as Sadie.

Rosita had eyes like pools of water that drowned me. I could see myself in her every time she came up against me for a kiss. We had our share. Not that I ever took her any place.

Sadie never said a word, nor did she follow us around. Rosita lived in a rent house we had. I was not old enough to drive a car by myself that year. Her father was there seismographing for El Paso Natural, or one of those other big companies. Come to think about it, it was probably Union or Texaco. El Paso did big ditching jobs, mostly.

One day I caught Sadie and Earnest 'round behind the gym after a basketball game. He had her up against him like she was a glove he was trying to put on. Before I knew it, I hit him. It was not like that other time. Earnest mopped the playground up with me. He left me half dead.

Funny thing about it, Sadie stayed with me after the fight was over. "Hank," she said. Tears fell down across her face, "I thought you had forgotten me."

Bloody and dazed as I was, I had sense enough to bring her down close to me. We kind of half sat there in the sand and loved each other. "You do not know how much you hurt me going with Rosita. She is so much prettier than me. Oh Hank," she said in a voice that tore me all to pieces, "do not ever leave me again."

When we finally got decent and went back inside to the dance, Earnest was close dancing with Rosita. I mean closer than two of us had ever danced. I took Sadie in my arms and was not jealous again. She was mine.

Even when we were real little children, whenever both of our families got together, the two of us always wandered off somewhere and made mud pies or played guns. Sometimes she could get me to play house with her. I was always the daddy. We knew each other better than most married couples ever know each other.

That spring we went down to Portales for senior orientation. Both of us fell in love with Eastern. It was so wide open and friendly. Even the teachers treated us like human beings. What I am saying is, we did not go there because it was convenient. There were some other schools 'bout as close. The University of New Mexico was just over the mountain. Then there were several Texas schools close by, plus New Mexico Highlands, which both of us liked because it was close to the mountains.

The people of Eastern were friendly and both of us were given rodeo scholarships that made up our minds. We were going there come fall. It was funny about both of us, once we made up our minds to do something, we did it whole hog.

We shopped together, making sure we bought clothes with a lot of Eastern's colors, green and silver, in them. Sadie looked real nice in a green sweater and a silver skirt. Of course, it was too hot for her to wear them late in the spring.

They took us to Ruidoso for our senior trip, three days of hiking through mountains. Snow was all gone, so skiing was out. There were so many things to do. Some of us fished for trout in a little stream. It ended up in our going almost skinny-dipping. Sadie would not let me look until she got all the way in the water. She claims she turned her head when I ran and dove in. I never believed her.

There was a bunch of people all around, so we did not have any privacy. Teachers kept checking on us, staying far enough back not to break into our privacy, but still close enough to keep us from openly doing anything real good. They did not come around while we were swimming, but they were visible enough, we knew they were there. Besides, that mountain water was too cold for us to get carried away. Real cold.

Goose bumps on blue skin are not attractive. We did not even bother to hide when we came out and got dressed. Sadie let me hold her soon as she got on her briefest underthings. It was not very sexy, cold as we were.

Some people would probably say we were not normal kids, keeping from going all the way like that. You would have to understand we loved and respected both ourselves and our parents. Kids were doing it all around us. We knew it, but the two of us could be together all day and half the night and come back without having gone all the way. Maybe it was not normal, but we liked it that way.

We were not prudes, either. Probably no other couple in school stayed together as much as we did. Except when we were playing sports or something, we were together. Teachers tried to separate us our first year in school. They gave up. We gravitated towards each other like magnets. It was not a brother-sister combination either.

"Hank," she said one day before graduation, "Why don't we enter the rodeo up at Durango this summer?"

They have a big one up there every year in July or August. I mean it is a big one, with top riders coming from all over. If a football player or baseball player goes to playing for money, he is out as an amateur. A rodeo rider can ride both ways and still do collegiate rodeoing. The only way a bunch of southwestern boys go to school is riding for money in summer.

I mean they make some big money. They have big, new pickups capable of pulling a trailer with a cutting horse in it. There at Eastern, people around town make a living boarding college students' horses. Sadie and I had already made plans to take a string of horses with us.

You should not get the wrong impression of me. I lived on some pretty poor land, but we had money. Dad had put together and inherited something over fifty sections of land. You start figuring a section as being one mile square, and you have a large spread of land. It took more than a day to drive a pickup over all that land. No one would think about walking that far.

We had some gas and oil leases bringing in some money on top of cattle, which we broke even with some years and other years we made a fortune. We kept most of our steers until they were full grown. Some of those herds we shipped from Nara Visa's stockyard would fill up a train. When prices were good, we cleaned the range out. When prices were poor, we kind of sat on them until we could do better. We were not hurting, even after this hard winter.

All of us bought lots of cake and made those cattle stomachs burn until they would go out and eat that dry grass. They would fill out with water enough that they would stay in pretty good shape most winters. Spring was when they really put on their weight. We could fatten them out real slick by June.

We were not poor people living from hand to mouth. I still drove my old, blue pickup, but it was because I wanted to rather than because I had to.

Dad promised to let us use his pickup for Durango. My old truck was plenty good enough to rodeo in close to home. My main event was bull riding, but most of the time I did some roping. Only way a rodeo man could make any money roping was to have a good horse he had trained himself. True, a few have made it riding someone else's horse, but very few.

A roper had to have a horse he could break out on and trust that horse like it was his wife. Same way with barrel riding, which women did. Those ladies had to have horses that would lay down going 'round those barrels. A person working with horses could get awful broken up riding someone else's horse.

Take a bull rider, he does not ever get to train his bull. Some riders may draw the same bull a time or two, but they never count on it. You take those bull riders, it looks real dangerous. If a man plays his cards right, it is no worse than any other sport. Thing to do is outsmart the animal. Worst thing a man can do is run from the bull after he's off. Best thing to do is let the clown come in and take all the danger. They are paid and trained for that. Riders are not.

Most of us learned to ride and rope out on the range. Dad never did like for me to practice on his stock, but he could not watch everything that went on all the time. I started riding calves with Sadie and Earnest almost as soon as the three of us could walk. Dad used to sit me on bull calves that were still sucking their mothers.

Earnest was from town. His father taught math at the high school. Perhaps riding bulls and horses is inborn in ranch people. Earnest never learned.

There is a feeling of oneness when a person mounts a bucking horse and stays with it until the last buck. Sitting there, not only trying to stay on, but to remember that it is necessary to make points by making certain moves during the bone-jarring ride, that is rodeoing.

As much as a rider feels he is a part of a horse, riding a bull is different. Why did I ride? Did you ever go to an amusement park and ride the tilt-a-whirl? Riding a bull is much better. You get on two thousand pounds of raw meat that is turning every way but loose. It is like putting your life against a cyclone and winning.

I never thought I would lose my seat. It was like I was a part of any animal I rode. Somehow, I learned that if a person watches ears and heads of animals, he can predict pretty well what an animal is going to do. If a rider cannot learn to predict his animal's movement, he had better leave the arena.

With Sadie it was different. We talked about it. She not only thought of herself as part of her horse while she cut 'round barrels, trying to beat out other contestants, but she enjoyed the noise and bright lights when she rode dangerously close to the ground.

We picked up a little money locally. Not much, but enough to buy a new stock trailer so that we could haul our horses tandem. It was a fancy job with covering over the horses in case it rained. We were ready for Frontier Day in Durango.

CHAPTER
TWO

Both our fathers decided to take off and go with us. First, Mother decided to go, then Sadie's mother said she would enjoy the mountains, even though she could not stand watching her daughter ride.

Sadie and I rode together in Dad's new pickup, while our parents drove 'long with us in a Cadillac Dad wanted to try out before he bought it. We cut over the mountains to Bernalillo and then drove up through Cuba to Aztec. The trip up the Animas River took all my driving skills when the trailer swayed around switchbacks.

We came out of one hundred degree-plus heat into a cool eighty degrees. Sadie moved over close to me, seeking comfort on these roads that wound around the mountains, giving us a view of water hundreds of feet below. It was hard to keep my mind on the road.

It was a good thing the pickup had a compound low gear, otherwise we would have never made it up some of those hills without unloading and leading the horses. It was that close to stalling out coming over some of those mountains.

We arrived three days early. Easiest way to kill a horse is to bring it into that high altitude straight off the New Mexico plains. Thinner oxygen content will knock them deader than a gun. Their hearts give out.

A person will do the same thing, but not as rapidly. Sadie and I checked into a motel. Four of us had reserved adjoining rooms. We pretty well lived together those three days, while we took time to see some of Colorado's beauty.

Smelling pine trees and mountain streams was enough for Sadie and me. We were much freer with each other. It was like graduating from high school was a milestone that gave us a passport to being adults. Even though I was free to drink alcohol, with Dad buying, I did not care to take a swallow.

Sadie and I took the pickup and went up some little river valley, way up to the top, where there had been gold mines. Even though some old buildings and equipment remained, we saw no signs of life. Oddest part was that there were ricks of wood still stacked as if any day, miners might come back and fire up.

The mountains brought Sadie and me closer together. It was a new dimension, where even our basic drives were sharpened by the clear mountain view. There were places we could see out across Colorado, even down into New Mexico, forty or fifty miles away.

It is strange how changing scenery can heighten a desire for each other. I held her in my arms so many times that day it would have been impossible to count. She clung to me and we never did grow tired of each other.

"I love you, Sadie," I whispered gently to her. "No matter what, I will stay with you, my Darling."

"Oh, Hank, how are we going to go on living like this? Maybe it would be better for us to marry before we go down to college."

"It might seem better now, but we would have children first thing, and you won't get through school. We will make it."

I loved her more that summer than I had ever loved anything or anybody in my life. We enjoyed each other's touch and smell. I ran my nose through her hair, smelling its cleaness. She put her hands around me and brought me close. I drew her into my body. Her warmth brought both of us together and then apart.

She was everywhere that day. We raced through mountain pastures where blue iris bloomed. We chased up strange animals that neither of us recognized. We explored old cabins and mine shafts filled knee-deep with water.

We ate our lunch spread out on odd-smelling ferns and other flowers. It was as if that day would never end. We willed the sun to stand still. She threw her head back and lay on the soft grass. I moved beside her. It was like we were the only two people alive in a primeval world where time stood still.

"Oh, Hank, let's don't go back. We could restore one of these cabins and live here together, forever."

"Winters are awful cold up here. Man told me snow gets twenty feet deep."

"We could lie and make babies all winter. Oh, Hank, I love you so much."

It felt good hearing her say it. An agreement with a mother is something I did not take lightly. Sadie knew that, perhaps that was why we could be so free and open with each other without being afraid of the consequences. We were more than two who had grown up sharing each other's thoughts. We were two people who knew each other in such a way that our brains were fused together.

We came off the mountain before dark. It was peaceful being surrounded by pine trees and aspen, with Christmas tree spruce up higher on the mountainsides. We stopped in at the little store for Cokes and learned that the river was called La Plata, The Silver; it was also the name of the county. There was a total feeling of a higher being that pervaded the Colorado countryside. For people from New Mexico's plains, it was like being in another world.

New Mexico is not without beauty, even over where I lived. It was a more subtle beauty; a drawing of velvet down over rough range grass, seeing red in rocks and appreciating looking over vast areas of land with the eye of an explorer; this was my heritage.

We went to church on Sunday, but we were not the butt picking good people on down around Portales. The farther south you get, the more religion becomes an outward thing, with people trying to appear holy. In Nara Visa, we were religious when it came to helping each other, but we did not go 'round all the time trying to show other people how religious we were.

The times when we were most religious were when we thought we could see God's handiwork in nature. Looking off over real estate and seeing touches of gold and silver in a sunset made me realize there was an owner and creator of this real estate besides myself. It is important to my story that you understand how we felt.

The fact that Sadie and I spent a day together enjoying ourselves and the mountains without actually having physical sex did not mean we were so religious, it was just our code. Sadie's mother asked us to wait until we married before we went all the way, and that was the way we lived. Some people might have thought we were foolish, but we did not. I guess we had about as much fun as most.

All the next day was rodeoing. There was a big parade. Sadie, on her black, led the way. I rode flank on some big shot. Whether it was a senator, governor, parade master or what, I did not ask. Most of those fat asses in office cannot ride a horse after they have been in an office seat for more than a month.

It was a perfect day. Blue sky, sun beaming down, but cool in comparison to New Mexico. We started at the south side of town and rode up Main Street with flags fluttering in the breeze.

Only a person who has ridden in a rodeo parade will know what I mean. It was like being in a fairy world with only the people lining the sidewalks being real. Durango is a red brick town with a dinky little railroad coming down from Silverton. When I was there, it was nothing more than a tourist line, but years ago it had been the lifeline in and out of this river valley.

Like I said, Sadie sat her prancing horse like a true queen. Her golden hair cascaded down her back. She was dressed all in red, white and blue, with her Stetson and rodeo boots providing the white. She sat her horse like she was glued on it. I am not getting across how beautiful that day was. Tall mountains all around, those old brick buildings and that little, dinky, shiny train blowing its whistle, while we rode proudly up to the rodeo grounds. I was proud of her, prouder than I can ever tell.

Soon as we had a chance, we went and checked the bull I had drawn. He was a brute. Dark brindle, his name was Diablo, which means Devil. He lived up to his name.

"You have to ride that thing, Hank?"

"Guess so, Sadie. One I drew."

"Look at him. His eyes are the meanest part about him."

"I never look at a bull's eyes."

"Why?"

"They gain control over you that way."

"You do not mean that, do you?"

"Sure I do. Did you ever notice a rabbit? He will sit perfectly still without moving. Hidden. When he sees your eyes, he will run. Same way with any other animal, look at their eyes, they will scare you."

"Hank, you are teasing."

"No I am not, Sadie. Reason people want you to look in their eyes when they are talking to you is because they want to intimidate you. Best way is to look at them, but do not see their eyes."

We were standing there before the bull pen, holding hands, carrying on this intellectual conversation just like we were in a fancy restaurant. Eastern people say us bull-riding westerners do not have class, but we do, only different things turn us on. Why is looking at a Van Gogh in a stuffy art gallery any more stimulating than looking at a mean bull in a bull pen?

You take ol' Diablo, he had those wicked, black horns that, with a little bit of imagination, a person could see red blood streaked on the black. Take his lines, clean cut like a Greek statue. Put a man on one of those things, you had one of those mythical things where a man's body comes out of a bull's torso. It takes a little imagination.

"I am hungry, Hank. Let's go find our parents and eat."

"Sounds good. Know where they are?"

"Mother said they would be up at that place that looks like a railroad car."

"What are we waiting for?"

I spun the pickup out on soft gravel, which caused a Durango policeman to cast a disapproving glance my way. Seeing I had the rodeo queen in with me, he threw a friendly wave with a "Watch it," which I could not hear through my rolled-up window.

Main Street was clogged clear up to Animas City. People were in Durango from all over to see some good riding and roping. I could see it was going to be a sellout.

I did not mind riding a bull on our back acres, but it was never the thrill of sitting on one before a crowd of thousands of cheering people, who would have liked nothing better than to see me have a bull horn stuck in my groin. People are like that. It must be the animal in them.

It gave me a great deal of pleasure the way people stepped aside when we walked into that strange looking place. Some of them recognized her as the queen. She had been on the front page for two days. It was her beauty and the way she carried herself that caused people to step aside.

Me, I will dress the part when it comes to church or founder's day. When I am working a rodeo, it is different. It is another job to me. A good western shirt with fancy buttons, a faded pair of Levi's, old comfortable boots and a white Stetson bent to shape was all I needed. Some riders put little black neckerchiefs 'round their necks. All it did for me was cut off my air.

"You two have a good time yesterday?"

"You should have come with us, Mother. Hank took me way up a river valley where there was only a dirt road going up a mountainside. Beautiful." I was glad Sadie liked it.

We ordered chicken-fried steaks all around. Both our fathers had a pulling match trying to get the ticket. Mother finally wound up with it after all the show was over.

No one would have recognized me as one of the best bull riders in the United States. The way I was headed, it was going to be Madison Square Garden this season. No one would have thought of me being a rodeo star, because most people expected a champion rider to be much older and bigger. I did not weigh over 140. Being fresh out of high school did not give me credibility. No one paid me much attention, except for Sadie and her mother.

My father and mother did not catch eyes. Nor did Sadie's father. They were plain dressing people you would find in any western town.

Dad wore a freshly ironed pair of Levi's, a good pair of boots and a western shirt, light red-plaid with white, not gaudy. A yellow Bull Durum tag always hung out of his pocket. Anytime he had to deliberate, he always pulled that bag out and carefully rolled him a cigarette. Mother kind of frowned at him, but he did not seem to mind.

Sadie's father was a little mouse-eared man who dressed a little fancier than my father. He always wore gabardine and some kind of fancy shirt. His boots were what caught your eye. He must have had a dozen pair made from exotic animal skins. The ones he had on today were crocodile. Some of his more unusual ones were causing people to carry signs that said save the gazelle, or some other rare animal.

Mother dressed about the same as Sadie's mother. But neither one of those women was flashy that was where the similarity ended.

The view out that big window we were seated by was worth looking at, but we did not stay at our table long as we would have liked. People were lined up out to the street.

It is never a good idea to stand around before a rodeo and worry. It will whip you every time. You will come out with sweaty hands and butterflies in your belly.

"Hank, I need to go back to our motel for a minute."

I did not ask why. All I did was spin the wheels and make a wide arc out onto Main Street and head back towards where we were staying.

We went inside and Sadie said, "Hank, hold me a minute. I have a case of jitters." There is nothing I enjoyed more than curing a case of Sadie's nerves. She could be most passionate during those spells. We barely stopped before it was time for us to be at the rodeo grounds for the grand entrance.

This time, people stood aside when we went to mount our horses. A rodeo queen at a rodeo is looked upon about the way the Queen of England is at a full dress affair, only the Queen is not quite as revered.

I have ridden bulls, and I have run the mile in a track meet. To me, running the mile takes more endurance. Anyway, I psyched myself up by pretending I was going to a track meet instead of a rodeo performance. It always calmed me down.

There is nothing more unglamorous than running in a track meet. They are always held on the coldest spring day of the year.

Why they insist on running them in skivvies, I will never know, unless women come to see some blue-legged, frozen runner break a little piece of paper tape. I could have been turned on better by staying home and watching Dad lay around the house in an old pair of boxer shorts.

We finished the opening entrance while everyone awed over Sadie. It was only when I escorted her up to the grandstand that I could hear whispers of "Who is that runt?"

It started with a blast and never let up. Four clowns cavorted out in front of people, while different events were getting ready. You have probably been to rodeos where people get bored sitting and waiting for the next event. You know the kind, little boys get down under the bleachers and look up ladies' dresses and then get all excited before they have a real scuffle with some other little boy. This never happened at the Durango rodeo.

Sadie won first place in barrel racing, which brought a big cheer from the crowd. I breezed through all the other events. In calf roping, my time was less than half of everybody else's.

Finally, it came time to swing up on the chute and wait to drop down on Diablo. I knew if I lasted through this one, the rest of the rodeo would be easy. They never let you ride the same animal twice. Those other bulls looked like Bambi beside the monster I had to master.

They called my name out real loud. I lowered myself down on that bull and grabbed the cinch with one hand, like you are supposed to do. There was a television station in town that day, and I caught my ride late that night, after the evening performance. If there was ever a perfect ride, it was that one. My left hand stuck out perfectly. I spurred that bull and put on the best performance of my life. I tried not to show it, but I was proud of myself, the way that ride went. Only thing that marred it a little bit was that I lost my hat when the pickup man came to get me. That was before the clown came running out to get that snorting bull off me. If the clown had not jumped in a big padded barrel, he would have been killed.

I even tried to look noble when I picked myself off the ground and dusted my pants real professional like.

Rest of the show was a piece of cake. The crowd went wild when I went out to accept my belt buckles. There were some big names at that show, and I walked away with it. There were some unhappy looks on faces when I went up to the judges' platform. "First time a kid not even dry behind the ears ever beat me," one of the biggest names muttered loud enough for me to hear.

We drove out early the next morning. It would have been perfect, except coming down a mountain by Cedar Hill, the trailer hitch broke. It was not my fault. It must have been a poor job of manufacturing.

Sadie called out, "Watch it, Hank. We are going to be killed." That was before the trailer out ran us down the steep road. If I had not run into the side of the mountain, it would have gotten me. It did kill Sadie's big, black stallion, but my cutting horse was not hurt. Sadie went all to pieces. That horse was given to her when it was a colt.

Our parents had been slow getting off. They came creeping down 'round those switchbacks 'bout the time I led my horse back out of the valley. It made me sick to look, but Sadie's horse had a thin trickle of blood coming out of his nostrils. There was no other mark. He must have broken his neck.

It was well into the afternoon before we could fill out all the accident reports and find another trailer. None of us was going to lose money on the deal. Sadie's horse was insured for ten thousand, which was not enough for a good barrel running horse. It really made me feel good when the insurance adjuster wrote up the report blaming the trailer manufacturer for the accident.

There was a jagged break where the trailer tongue had parted company. All I needed was for Sadie to blame me for the rest of my life for killing her horse. Things like that are pretty important to us rodeo people.

We made it back to Nara Visa the next day. It was embarrassing; they had a welcoming committee waiting on the highway there where you come into town. They honked their horns and cheered us when we finally stopped for a cup of coffee. I noticed my picture on the Albuquerque paper that was enclosed in one of those little boxes you stick a quarter in, and the lid falls down.

The rest of that summer went by real fast, with me trying to rodeo and ranch, while at the same time get ready for college.

Dad rode up on me one day while I was trying to pull a cow out of a bog with a horse that would no more cooperate than a mule. I was covered with mud from wading in that quicksand, trying to get as good a hitch on her as possible. If Dad had not helped out, we never would have gotten that old heifer out of that bog hole.

After we got her tits washed off enough so her calf could suck, we sat down and talked a spell. Dad had one of his roll-your-owns going before we had even washed our hands.

"Know what you are going to do after you finish school, Hank?"

"Thought I would come back here and take over. You will need help by then."

"I hoped you would say that. Sometimes after a day in the saddle, my leg gets to hurting me a right smart. Don't know how much longer I can hold out. Sadie's daddy and I talked about building you two a big house between ours. You will have a lot of land someday, son. Both of these ranches take in most of this end of Quay County."

We talked on, father to son talk. I gathered he loved me a great deal. But, I knew that already. Only time I had been really mad at him was when he had taken my driving privileges away. I had forgotten 'bout that a long time ago.

"You will not make it home much, football this fall and rodeoing. Your mother and I are going to miss you. College is going to be different. You are going to have to buckle down with all the things you are going to do - the Garden and all those stock shows you are signed up to ride in. You are smart. It will work out."

Dad did not show much emotion, but there were tears in his eyes that time when we stood up to ride back home. That was the last time we really talked.

CHAPTER
THREE

Sadie and I drove down through eastern New Mexico's dry plains two days before Eastern opened its fall semester. It was going to be difficult with one old pickup for the two of us, but her parents did not think she should have a car until she settled in.

When we went into the Registrar's Office to find out where we were going to stay, I did not like the way one big goon looked at her. She pulled on my arm.

"Hank, you cannot fight every man who gives me a lecherous look. Besides, what are you doing looking at other girls?"

I started to protest my innocence. There was no use, she knew me better than I knew myself. "I am not blind just 'cause we are promised."

"I never heard you promising anything, Hank. All you want to do is put your hands on me."

"You never protest."

"Maybe I like it. It would be nice if you would once in awhile talk to me instead of always grabbing."

"You know how I feel."

"Can I help you?" the secretary asked.

We continued to carry on our private conversation.

"Excuse me. Are you two married?"

"No. Why?" I asked crossly.

"You are acting like my husband does, that is why. Now, we have a number of students coming in here. How about telling me what you want."

She was a motherly type lady with glasses. "All you have to do is tell me what you want and perhaps I can help you. They pay me to do that."

I asked her where we were to stay. "Hank, you are here on athletic scholarships. You will stay over by the gym. Sadie, you go down to the girls' dorm. Here is a map. You are not far from either place. Are you walking?"

I assured her we had transportation. "Do you mind if we look around?"

"No, of course not. There are interesting paintings on the wall. Look at them when you walk upstairs. They are from Proverbs. W.P.A. workers painted them during the depression. They represent youth and old age. The artist wanted to remind youth not to waste their time. We try to emphasize that message here."

She gave us a map of the campus and welcomed us to Eastern. We walked upstairs and looked at murals on the walls. They brought a lump to my throat; I thought about all the students who had been reminded of opportunities of youth, and how it could be wasted.

Sadie dug me in the ribs. "Mind telling me what you are so serious about?"

"Thinking."

"That is unusual for you."

I took her hand and helped her up the rest of the steep stairs. All the second floor was classrooms. The well-lit rooms smelled of chalk dust and newly waxed floors. We stood looking out the north window.

"Says that is the Student Union Building," Sadie said, while we stood looking at a building with a balcony all along the second floor. "Let's go see it."

"I thought you wanted to look through this building."

"Changed my mind. Besides, there are a bunch more buildings. Come on, Hank. Let's explore."

We walked in the front entrance of the building across the narrow street. It was interesting, formal parlor, next a coffee shop and then a quadrangle surrounding an enclosed area with patio furniture and umbrellas. "I am hungry. How about you?"

We took our sandwiches out on the patio and ate. Everything

was so different. We sat over our malts looking at the campus map we had been given. Every department had a different building. There was the science and humanities building. We had an argument over what humanities meant. We later found out neither one of us was right.

There was a book store, a game room, and a large formal ball room with an orchestra pit on the north wall. "Will you?" I asked her.

While we whirled on the slick floor, an imaginary orchestra played music. All of a sudden there was music. An employee had turned on a speaker that gave us piped in music. This was going to be a new experience. Music in a school.

"Come on," I said. "I want to find the Ag building."

We spent our first afternoon hand in hand walking over the campus. I can still remember the first day on that large campus. There was the gym in an old Air Force building that had been moved over from Clovis. The Ag building was a temporary wooden building that did not impress me. Most Ag buildings are that way. Somehow, Ag Departments are last to get funds for new buildings and such.

After that depressing experience, we went back to the Student Union Building and danced again. There were twenty or thirty couples dancing to any kind of music those in control decided to play. Some of it was country western, but some was not. Eastern had some real hippies in those days, which was a shock to Sadie and me. We thought it was un-American to wear anything but western cut clothes.

What I am going to tell you next is going to turn some of you off, and you may stop reading. Religion does that to people who read books. I started to leave it out, but what I am writing about made headlines all over Texas and then it got on T.V. I have to explain. This is not just a cheap romance about a cowboy trying to get in a coed's pants. I admit it was on my mind all the time, but most young men my age to whom I have talked are about the same way.

The older I get, the more I find out that old geezers up to ninety are after the same thing. It is a subject not researched by scientists. People will not tell the truth about their sex lives. Either they will tell you it is none of your damn business, or they will make up fantasies that will singe your hair.

Only way you can get the truth is be a psychiatrist or use drugs. Then they will lie or fantasize. I have listened to my share of sex confessions. Some of them are good, but most of them are not true.

How are you going to prove if a sex story is true? Usually it is between two people. I know there are groupies, but even in a groupie, only two people are actually in contact, and only one person is having the sex experience. There is no way another person can tell what you are experiencing. Maybe when we have electronic machines that will record human experience, then we can do a better job of finding out what goes on in the human mind. I hope I am dead when that happens.

Church groups spend large sums of money to recruit college kids. Do not be fooled. They use sexual attraction, food, games, reading, you name it. Do not think I am not an expert because my parents raised me on a ranch. This is enough; let me tell my story.

They were having open house at all the Chairs of Religion. From what I have been telling you about the two of us, you might think we are heathens without any religious experience.

You will notice I am not using last names. I am doing it to protect those who do not want publicity. What happened was big newspaper stuff for two months or more. In fact, five years later, things still crop up.

One of the professors over at the Baptist Chair of Religion had been up to Nara Visa supplying in our church. Baptists are not like some other denominations, they use young people training for religious careers to preach. Eastern's Baptist students go all over several states holding service. Most of them are lay people training for other professions.

Sadie and I listened to these groups in our church and in others. We had especially liked the young professor who had come up to hold services when our church had a big fight. I mean there was a slugging match. One member got up and clobbered the preacher.

Only our parents knew what had happened for sure.

"Hank," Sadie said, after we danced for over an hour, "let's go over to visit the Baptist Student Union Building."

Like most males, I did not take big to religion. Maybe it is because us males do not handle our sexuality as well as women, but we do not like religion. I have had a lot of time to think about it since, but did you ever notice women will tell each other the most intimate things about their sex lives? Some men will also, but most of it is a lie.

"I do not want to go."

"Why not, Hank? I've gone everywhere you wanted to go today."

"Thought you wanted to see where we are having classes."

"I did, but you led the way." She was that way when she wanted her way. She would always turn things around so I would be at fault. It did not bother me much because I loved her.

We ended up going over across the south campus to some private buildings where the Baptists had built a fairly attractive brick building. It was one of the few buildings with a good lawn. Eastern was growing so rapidly, people tore up lawns faster than they could grow grass.

There was a small crowd drinking punch and visiting quietly. Most of them were couples. Some were holding hands. Others were sitting in the parlor quietly visiting about what had happened to them during the summer. We were the only freshmen in the building.

"Baptists ever let couples dance, they will have a bunch more students in here."

"Hank, be quiet," Sadie whispered. "They think it is sinful."

"It is not."

About that time, a grown-up came up and introduced himself as Doctor. Said he was director of the facility, and head of the religious department. He was real good at finding out about us without asking questions. Of course he recognized me after we talked awhile. After all, I had been front page news all summer with all my rodeoing.

Another thing, I was the only one in there in western clothes.

Everyone else was in more traditional dress. I still had my Stetson on. The director casually showed me a hat rack.

There were older students who tried to corner Sadie and me to try and convert us. We steered clear of any real contact, but we did promise to attend evening vespers. They had a real attractive chapel that was well done in rich colors.

Sadie and I finally got away. We walked back across campus and got the pickup and took her clothes into the girls dorm, which was real close to the Baptist building. "I'll be back in a little while, and we can go eat."

"Where are you going, Hank?"

"Unpack my clothes."

"I am afraid."

"What is there to be afraid of?"

"It is so different, Hank. This is first time I have been away from home without you being here with me. I wish we'd gotten married."

"Let's go."

"Our parents would not like that."

There was not any use standing in the foyer to Eastern's girl's dorm and arguing about whether we should marry. It seemed everyone was all ears.

I was playing it real cool. My tires had not squealed even once, 'though I had forgotten myself once and raced a yellow sport car. I drove over to the athletic dorm.

There was a bunch of jocks standing around in front of my dorm. Most of them wore clothes that showed their muscles. Some wore gym shorts but no shoes.

The varsity had been on campus for a month practicing for their first game. Freshman had not been invited for preliminaries. I was the only one in both rodeo and football. Some in baseball caps stared at my western garb.

My roomie was lying on a cot similar to mine. He got up when I came in. All he had on was a pair of skivvy trunks. They were a grayish color from bad laundering.

He stuck out his hand, "I am Kent."

"Hank's mine."

"Read about you."

"Don't let it bother you. I can hang on a bull good is all."

"Want to go out and eat after you unpack?" Kent asked.

"Sorry, I have a date."

"Lucky one," he told me.

"We grew up together."

"I'm from Aztec," Kent said.

"How did you get past Albuquerque?"

"Not good enough for the University." The University of New Mexico was the "University," to distinguish it from the Ag school at Las Cruces and the other state and Catholic schools.

"End?" I asked. His tall, slender frame was not built for either a lineman or a back.

"Wouldn't you know. Guess where you have glue on your britches, I have glue on my hands."

"You the one who caught all the passes for Aztec three years ago when they went to state?" I asked.

"Guilty as accused. Where you from? Should know."

"Nara Visa," I told Kent.

"I would not brag about it."

"Aztec does not look much better. Went through there rodeoing at Durango this summer."

"Heard about it. All 'round winner, weren't you. Dad and I drove up," Kent said.

"Killed a horse at Cedar Hill, belonged to my fiance. Tough accident."

"Insured?" he asked.

"They paid right off after they found out how much Sadie made off barrel racing."

"Looks like I won't see much of you with a steady."

"I have a pretty busy year planned. Have to start footballing tomorrow, plus rodeo team."

"First time I have ever heard of a student doing both."

"They are going to let me try. It should not interfere with anything but my studies."

"You planning on studying? I am a three sport man myself."

"Forward?" I asked.

"Pitcher, also. Ran the mile in track," Kent said.

"We ought to see who's fastest. That's my race."

I could see Kent and I were going to be friends. He was from one of New Mexico's first Anglo families. There were a few of us whose families had been natives for four generations.

"Sorry to interrupt this, but Sadie's expecting me."

"Care if I ride towards town with you?" Kent asked.

"Not at all. No car?" I asked.

"It's at a filling station getting greased."

"Come on, I will give you a ride all the way to town."

We circled out north and hit the highway. There was a big grain elevator with Worley painted all over it.

"Big people here," Kent mentioned.

"Looks like it," I said.

Portales stretched out along the railroad track. A sleepy town in a quiet part of New Mexico, it was real empty, with only a few townspeople on the street and several students headed for the show. Some were hand-holding couples. They reminded me to hurry back for Sadie.

We approached a Texaco station. "Car's in here, thanks. Don't wake me up when you come in," Kent said.

We laughed, and I drove off with my tires spinning on the pavement this time, since I was off campus.

Sadie scolded me for being late, but not much. That night we ate at a drive-in and then went out and necked for awhile. It was different setting out on a dark gravel road. It was the freest we had been with each other, even more than in the mountains.

It was getting late when Sadie said, "Dorm closes at eleven tonight."

"Why didn't you tell me?"

"You would have spent the time thinking how we could spend more time out."

I threw gravel getting back on the black asphalt. If it had not been for the lights shining in the distance, I would have been lost.

"Guess these time limits are going to keep us apart. Athletes have to be in by nine on week nights. Twelve on Saturday and Sunday," I told Sadie.

"Bet you'd better find time for me. There's some real good looking older men."

"Saw a few worthwhile women."

"Hank, you promised me."

"Promised you I wouldn't date. Looking is different."

We barely made it in. There were students all over saying good night. At Eastern, students could kiss good night longer than any place I have ever seen. Sadie and I locked our lips together until a maternal woman came out and chased the men away.

Sadie and I ate our meals together. We went to two classes together, and that was about it, except for library and an hour before she had to be in. We were apart three or four hours a day.

If they had not kept me so busy and hazed me so much, I would have gotten a big head. The thing that really made me mad was not those little green beanies we had to wear, it was when they shaved my head and left ENMU growing in tufts. Hell. You notice I do not cuss much like some young men my age, but that made me mad. It took all fall for my hair to grow out.

First thing I did off campus was get rid of that FISH cap and put on my cowboy hat. That beanie was the only thing I had ever worn besides a Stetson in my life.

Although Sadie and I both had our horses pastured out west of town, at first I only bull rode at events away from campus. It took too long hauling a roping horse. There were times that fall, I was flying to rodeos and then flying to football games.

They had planned on red shirting me so I could play four years after my freshman year. That was before the quarterback broke his leg the first game. The other two did not work out in the second game.

The third game, Kent caught three touchdowns that I threw him, one from the forty yard line. We were good. I am not sure if it was my throwing or his catching, but Sunday's headlines were big: "COWBOY THROWS WESTERN FOR LOSS." It really impressed them in Portales.

We won our conference that fall. Sadie and I were already making the rodeo team look good. Her dad and mother came down and drove her horse to rodeos for us. Sometimes I drove back while her dad rode back in the car with her mother. Most of the time, I had to fly somewhere or other.

This is how I got hooked on making speeches for the Life Service Band at the Baptist Student Union. The director took students on speaking engagements all over the state. It was good publicity for the Baptists to hold weekend revivals. Religious majors did the preaching, while lay students gave speeches about their religious experiences.

Sadie got real hep on the program. Pretty and popular as she was, organizations all over campus sought after her. Only reason Baptists did not rush us at first was because we danced. A dancing Baptist is like a duck out of water. They swore a person could not dance and be a Christian.

We argued about this a lot, Sadie and the other Baptist students. They finally left us alone after they saw they could not change us. Especially when they found out that our names on their program drew those west Texans and New Mexicans in droves. My name was a byword. Sadie's was right behind mine.

It got to where they flew me to religious rallies. I spoke and flew other places for rodeoing or football without even hearing any of the program.

I have always liked to be in the center of things. Probably that is the way they hooked me on speaking. You know by now that I was not a Holy Joe type. All I did was tell how I thought the Christian way helped me win.

This was what most of those high school students wanted to hear. Nothing interested them but making out with girls and making touchdowns, in that order. If they could get the Lord on their side, so much the better. I tried to tell them how to make touchdowns. Sometimes it sounded like the Lord and I had a partnership that made that ball go right into Kent's arms every time I threw it.

Do not make me out to be a religious fake. I was not. I believed in kids growing up free of liquor and drugs. If religion made them better people, that was all right with me. Only thing, it took Sadie 'till Tuesday after one of those religious meetings before she could really be free with herself again.

Only thing I have against religion, it tries to take the place of sex. There is not anything in my experiences that will take that place. Not even Mexican food, which I enjoy more than anything else.

Anyway, we finally overcame religion and were able to enjoy each other again within our boundaries, rather, her boundaries. Religion was not making me any less willing to take everything Sadie would give me.

We were the most popular couple in the freshman class. I was elected president, and she secretary. They used us for every charity drive in the state that year. I do not mean the little ones, but the real big ones up at Albuquerque and Santa Fe.

A football scout came from the University and tried to sign me up for the next year's football season. They offered me everything from a new car to a different girl in my bed every night, none of which was legal. Do not kid yourself, there is not a legal football alumnus in the United States. Even those real religious ones will think of things to corrupt a real good player.

It was a good thing for me Eastern had an alumnus living in Portales who was rich enough to have a Lear. How else do you think Sadie and I were able to fly around all over the state? He even hired a graduate student to fly with us and tutor us while we were away from campus.

Sadie was every bit as famous as I was, with her barrel racing. One of the real rich ones had her horse transported along with mine when they found out I could win roping as well as ride bulls. They would drive our horses up, fly us, then bring our horses back the next day.

We got so good, they started going after our parents in another Lear so we could see each other. One thing they insisted on was that we study. Eastern was strange. You had to pass. Way we were with private tutors and secretaries to type our papers, we were straight A students all the way through.

Do not get the idea that we did not study. Our tutors did not do the actual writing of papers. One or the other went over to the library and gathered up material for us. They marked pertinent passages, and typed it up after we roughed it in. The two of us put at least four graduate students through school every semester we were there.

CHAPTER
FOUR

The only reason I stayed at Eastern was because of their attitude. By my second year, every major school in the United States was after me for quarterback. If you want to see how good I was, dig out some of the sports magazines from that period. Sports writers were making almost as much on me as I was.

The people in the town, though, were too close for their own good. Some of them wanted to force their narrow views on every phase of university life. Just because I still will not touch beer does not make me want to force every other person to leave alcohol alone. It would be best if they did, but that is no business of mine.

One church asked Sadie and me to leave because we were observed on a dark country road by a mean-eyed little deacon. We were still both virgins, but neither of us cared to show our badges of virtue.

There were some other things, like in church, when deacons served communion. All the church members stood and people who were not stayed seated, so they could not partake. I stayed seated. Anyway, churches in that town never asked me to speak and that was fine with me.

I was talking about Eastern. Famous as I became, they never would let me move off campus. With Kent as a roommate, I did not want to go anyway. "Long as you play football here, Hank," the coach told me, "you are obeying our rules. Every football player not married lives on campus."

I did not argue. Besides, Sadie was a cheerleader so she could go to out of town games with us. We thought we would miss a lot of college life if we lived off campus. The people at that school showed a lot of understanding, even after all the trouble I got into after graduation. They still send me alumni magazines. When I go on campus, they give me V.I.P. treatment.

"Hank," Sadie told me about December, "we have not been home since we came down here. How about your driving me home this Friday after school?"

It turned out this was a good idea. Dad died while we were on our way home. We did not even know about it until we stopped by Sadie's house.

Her daddy met me at the door. "Hank, I have some sad news to tell you. Your father was out throwing range cubes and had a heart attack. Your mother could not get him to the hospital soon enough. He died in the cab with her driving."

It was like someone hit me in the pit of my stomach with a pickax. Sadie was holding me tight. Her ma came out crying hard. She threw her arms around me. "Son," she said, "we are so proud of you. It is such a bad thing to happen to such a good man. Let me phone your mother so she will know you are here."

We stayed until Tuesday before we went back to school. Mother needed me longer than that. We talked it over. "Hank, you have almost a lifetime ahead of you. Do not waste it staying here on this place. You found out that the world is a lot bigger than this place, big as it is."

"You cannot run it by yourself," I told her.

"Sadie's daddy wants to oversee both places. He is getting too old for everyday ranching. We'll hire some more help and split the profits. The two places will work in together real good."

Sadie and I talked it over for two hours before the funeral. We decided it was best this way.

When we buried Dad on Monday afternoon, it was a gray day with no sunlight. It was not raining either. The clouds set in low, keeping out most of the sun's light.

It seemed that the gloomy weather intensified my grief. If it had not been he talked to me the day before I went to the University, I do not think I could have stood it. It was not so bad in church, with all the flowers and things. When we stood out under that cloudy sky, and I saw that new dug grave, I just about went to pieces. If Sadie had not been there with me, I would. She held my arm while the minister told us how good a man Dad was. He knew Dad well.

There will never be as good a man anywhere as Dad. He never preached his goodness; he showed it. There never was a person who came to his house who went away hungry. We never saw him treat even a dog cruel. That night he took the pickup away from me, he was crying.

When they started throwing dirt on the grave, it was as if the world caved in. Before that, I still had hopes of him walking out of that coffin and going home with us. When they started the dirt, I knew there was no use hoping.

It was then I understood what the minister was saying about the resurrection and the life after death. It was then I had some inkling of what the whole Christian message was about. It was like Dad came from the dead and told me.

I went back to school with Sadie driving. I did not have the strength to try and keep my mind on the road ahead. We drove fifty miles when she pulled off down a side road. "Hank," she said. "I cannot stand seeing you like this. You never let anything get you down. I am going to take some pretty drastic action here. I am offering you my body, even though I wanted to wait for us to marry."

She came over and started undressing. I held her warm body in my arms. We sat there a long time. Finally I said, "I never could face your mother. You have given me more than most men ever get from a woman. I can wait."

"You are sure?" she asked.

"Yes."

"You scoot over here under this wheel then and drive. I cannot stand seeing you looking like that."

She came over against me. We had not driven five miles by the time she had her head against my shoulder asleep. We drove the last thirty miles with the dashboard lights shining their green, subdued light on her sleeping face. She was like an angel.

Most young men in my position would have found a willing woman and kept it from their girlfriend. Some of my friends went over to a house in Clovis every week or two. I never could explain about Sadie to anyone. Nor, did I ever try. All I knew was that she was mine, and I loved her.

It was our second year there when they brought a band leader in from Oklahoma University. No one ever learned what they gave him in return. Eastern would not make a dent in Oklahoma's enrollment.

I forgot his name. He wore his uniform like Napoleon leading his troops. He was a little taller than me, but not much. He had an act where he took batons and lit them. He would twirl those flaming things and juggle them out there on that field with all the lights out. He was so good, the coach let us stay out at halftime and watch.

That was the year Indiana U. had the golden girl. If any of you are old enough, you will remember her. She was a looker. They persuaded Sadie to take that position at Eastern. You will understand how beautiful she was, if you will believe she put the Indiana girl to shame. It was not just my opinion, either.

We were not under much pressure that year. It was then we won our first title as champion small collegiate school in the United States. We played that title game and I threw three touch-downs.

Sadie did not even let me get off the field. You know how it is after a football game, fans start leaving soon as they know who won. When she came out in her tights and threw her arms around me, everyone paused. Before she stopped kissing me, we had a standing ovation.

We walked across campus to breakfast. I always went with her. It was a ritual we repeated every morning we were there together.

"Hank," she said.

"Yes," I said.

"You know how that band leader has been helping himself to every available girl on this campus?"

"I heard stories. A girl told her mother before all the cafeteria that he had been taking her to the bushes."

"Last night, after you left, a tired young mother came leading two little boys and carrying a little boy in her arms. It is his wife, from Dennison, Texas," Sadie told me.

We laughed together. "At least I have not heard of any pregnant girls," Sadie said.

There was a quietness around campus all that week. It was as if every girl there had lost something personal. Even Sadie had a downcast look.

There were a few who said it was the Vietnam War that did it, but it was about that time I surrendered for full-time religious work. I cannot explain what happened. It was hard dropping out of the Ag program and starting in on a new major. I announced my decision before the whole student body at an assembly.

We had a president there who was a lay preacher. He was the greatest man I ever knew. Surely he will not mind if I name him, Dr. Floyd Golden. After Mrs. Golden heard about my decision, she came over and talked to me a long time.

She put her arm around me. "Hank," she said. "you have started on a hard road. You are young. Lots of things are going to happen to you that will try your faith. God can help you through them if you will let him."

"Only one thing worries me, Mrs. Golden," I paused. She waited a long time.

"What is it, Hank? Surely not Sadie."

"No. She is so happy. It is that I do not believe any church is above all others. I believe in Christianity and not in the Baptist way."

"Son," she said, "everyone believes that way sometime in their life. A person has to have some kind of framework to follow. Christianity has always traveled under man-made governments. Maybe after you finish your training, you will see things differently."

"Sadie and I have talked it over. We are going to continue going to school dances. You will still catch us out on some road nights."

"Good for you two. Never did think Christianity should emasculate a man. You go on living the way you are. We all admire you."

My decision did not make much difference in my life. Sadie and I kept our friends the way we had before. We lived with our classmates the same as we had always. Only thing different was I started preaching instead of just giving speeches. By this time you might think I am going to give you a lot of religion, but I won't.

I was a student officer in the R.O.T.C. The only thing I changed was that I was now a ministerial student, which would exempt me from the draft. The R.O.T.C. officer in charge discussed it. "Hank, go ahead and stay in the program. You may never use a commission, but the leadership program will be good for you."

I told Sadie, "I cannot stand these protesters. Our country is fighting. This is no time to be burning draft cards and protesting. A lot of fine men are giving their lives for us. We should be supporting them instead of hindering them."

Sometimes when I think about it, I feel that I did become a preacher to stay out of Vietnam. If there ever was a war mishandled, that one was. Think how many men gave their lives without winning. If we ever go into another war, we should go into it to win, and not play around.

Anyway, when I preached my first sermon it was at the coliseum in Fort Worth. They asked me because of my rodeo fame. There was not an empty seat in the place. Sadie sat up there on the podium with me.

It was a youth rally, but there were a lot of older folks there. Mother came down by herself.

I looked out over the sea of faces. There was not a sign of fear in me. My hands were as dry as they were when I was out on the range in a pickup. People were expecting more than I could deliver.

There was kind of the feeling I had when I looked at Diablo in Durango that summer so long ago. It was the same feeling before I swung over the chute's side onto the bull's back. I never looked at their eyes.

After I finished preaching, there was a mob-rush to the front. Over six thousand people were in that auditorium. Four thousand came forward. There were a thousand converts. The rest of the people repented of sins or dedicated their lives.

This was one time I did not wear a suit in a religious service. I did not even wear dress clothes. I preached that sermon in a pair of Levis and a fancy shirt. My boots shone. They did ask that I remove my Stetson.

Sadie and I went and looked at the Southwestern Baptist Seminary while we were there. The school impressed me with its big, beautiful buildings and spacious grounds. We made inquiries about living facilities, even though it would be over two years before we finished college. Sadie was elated. We stood under a bright Texas sun holding hands while we looked over the campus. When a stray beam of light lit up the chapel window, it was as if we had put our hands in God's hands.

The next two years went fast. Once again, my final year, we won the small school football title. We got beat out in the finals my junior year.

Every honor Eastern could bestow was given me. It was a heady last year. I still debated in religious classrooms whether the Baptist way was the only way. Little by little I was becoming more reconciled to the church I had chosen to work in.

It was the last collegiate rodeo I would ever ride in. Eastern's drill team was there with green and silver flags. Sadie won her barrel riding.

The bull I rode was even bigger and meaner than Diablo. There was a time, when I dug my spurs in, that I knew this was going to be my worst ride. Things did not go right on the first buck. The bull sun-fished. He stood on his head and then on his tail.

The crowd went wild while I rode that monster. We went around the whole arena twice, with the bull using all the tricks he knew, and I finally gained my seat more securely. It was a wild ride. I lost my hat again. The bull hit a post, and then he went for the clown.

There was no way I was going to drop off that mess. It was the first ride for me that lasted three times longer than it should have. Finally, the clown got back into the arena, and I dropped off when I saw he could handle the animal. It was a ride I would not have repeated.

When I went back to my place by the chute, where I tried to

staunch a bloody nose, a large man walked up to me and introduced himself.

"Hank," he started out, "we heard you are coming here to Texas for seminary. Sorry about that nosebleed. Can I finish?"

"Sure, go ahead. It will stop, I think."

"What we have in mind is for you to come over and pastor the First Baptist Church in Bulton while you're going to school."

"Bulton. That is where Texas Central's located, isn't it?"

"Yes. You beat out our bull rider here tonight. Central draws from a large range country. We are in hopes you can pull in most of the school. My name is Bill North."

"How big is your membership?"

"Four thousand."

"I can hardly handle that big a church and attend school."

"We want you strictly for preaching. We will hire someone else for visitation and administrative work. You willing to come and look us over?"

"Sure," I answered.

"It might interest you to know we have a new brick parsonage."

"We are planning to marry after graduation. That is my future wife who won the barrel riding," I told him.

"Yes, I know. We know more about you than you know yourself. Only thing we ask is that you do not preach your views on the church. What you believe is your business. Do not try to push it on us."

"Get in touch with me, will you? I am going to have to get some ice and stop this blood. It is about time to ride out and accept awards."

"Nice talking to you, Hank. Real nice."

I went over to find Sadie. She was good at stopping blood. It took time to work my way through the crowd. By the time I got to her, the blood stopped.

"Get your horse," she said. "We have to go. That was a horrible bull."

"I have some good news for you after this is over."

"I will be waiting to hear it." She smiled.

CHAPTER
FIVE

We rode circling the arena, carrying every state's flags even though there were only eight states there. It was an impressive thing with us riding three abreast. Sadie led the parade by herself.

"Ladies and gentlemen," the announcer said, "it is that time we have waited for all night. Now is the time to present the award for best all-'round cow girl. You have all guessed the judges' decision on that. Sadie, will you dismount and come to the judges table?"

I was proud when Sadie raced her horse in a hard gallop to the platform. Dismounting in a flying leap, she landed on her feet. When she proudly walked towards the judges, the crowd went wild. They came to their feet cheering when she approached. It had been a long afternoon and night, but it was coming to a close. I was still woozy from the loss of blood.

It was a grand finale, this honor and graduation next week. The flags were still while we sat in a circle opposite the judges.

"Ladies and gentlemen, while Sadie is coming up here, let me tell you this interesting bit of news. Sadie and Hank are graduating from Eastern New Mexico this spring. After all this time, they plan to marry. Sadie told me the two of them have gone together since they were in diapers. Both of them plan to attend Southwestern Baptist Seminary next fall. It will be Preacher for Hank after that. Let's give them a hand."

A thunderous ovation went up from the crowd. I was really feeling good. Life was starting all over for me. No longer did I dread being called Preacher.

There was a louder noise, above the roar of the crowd, when the bull I had ridden that evening hit his chute gate. He had been doing that ever since they had repenned him.

In most rodeos, they would have put the animals back in an enclosure, but they had trouble with this bull fighting the other stock, so they put him back in the same chute we came out for my championship ride.

There was a splintering of wood. Out came the bull, carrying most of the gate on his horns. He was a magnificent animal charging across the arena.

Sadie had not reached the judge's stand when he hit. All she needed was a second to reach safety. There was not time for her last step.

I sat paralyzed until too late. The bull pawed the ground and charged. It was as if she were a rag doll. The bull's horns still carried debris from the broken gate, or she would not have made it out of the arena alive. His blunted horns carried her fifteen feet at least. After she hit, he stood over her listless body pawing the ground before he hit her again. Still, he did not move off but continued to snort and bellow like he was checking to make sure she was dead.

I came alive. Throwing down New Mexico's sunshine flag, I raced towards the inert figure. The roaring crowd was instantly silent when I jumped from my horse and sought to divert that three-legged bull, who carried his fourth leg in a pawing stance off the arena floor.

We came at each other with no hesitation. "Take this one!" I did not have time to recognize the rider who threw me a flag. Waiting only to furl its bright colors out from me, I encouraged the raving beast to follow the rippling movements of my flag.

He charged directly at me, his horns still carrying a piece of gate. He came at my mid-section, but I side-stepped him. The massive rippling frame of bull went charging madly across the arena while I ran for Sadie's limp form.

Other cowboys quickly moved in and diverted the wicked animal towards a now-open gate. We were safe. The crowd hushed. I heard, "How brave. What happened?"

Not daring to move her broken body, I tenderly caressed what had been the body of a vibrant rodeo queen, checking for sure she still breathed. It was obvious though that she would never wear a wedding gown on our wedding day.

There was a screaming ambulance racing across the arena. Two men in white coats picked her up and expertly placed her on the stretcher. "Come on," they said, "we need you at the hospital. You kin?"

"Fiance," I said.

It was a mad dash across Fort Worth to the hospital. I did not see her again for eight hours. Twice they came out and told me she was dead, only to come back and tell me she was still fighting.

It was if someone had hit me with a sledgehammer twice. My thoughts were whirling like a broken television set with snow mixed in with dim figures.

They put her in intensive care with limited visiting hours. The hospital listed her condition as critical, with little hope of living.

I shuddered each time I stood over her wan face looking for some sign of recognition. She was not even able to respond with a simple flutter of her beloved eyelids. At times I thought there was no hope.

Her parents were there before nightfall. They flew from somewhere in Texas. The Dean of Students from Eastern came in shortly afterwards. A doctor in scrub greens asked us to come into his office.

After preliminary introductions, he turned to me. "There is very little hope of Sadie ever coming out of this coma. We counted eighty-two fractures to different bones. She has massive internal bleeding. If she lives, she may never recognize any of you again."

Her mother and father and I sat in sorrow after we heard the devastating message. "Hank," her mother said, "we will understand if you leave and never come back. Our little girl will not ever be fit for a bride."

"Mother, I will stay. She will live. She has to. I love her so much."

She opened her eyes ten days later. The first thing she saw when she struggled to focus her eyes were two dozen roses, which filled up her room. This was the third such bouquet I had brought her.

The doctor had not had a chance to visit her since she awakened. Her parents were out for coffee. It was my decision on what to tell her if she should ask questions.

Her first question was, "Will I ever walk again, Hank?"

I thought of the many times we had walked hand in hand across clumps of grama grass and rocks looking for newborn calves. There had been times we looked for arrowheads and pretty flowers. I wanted to say, "Of course you will walk again."

The spoken words were, "Sadie, it is very doubtful you will ever be able to even use a wheelchair. Can you move any part of your body?"

"Hank, these casts are pretty restrictive, but I can move the fingers on my right hand."

Her parents and the doctor came in to find me with my head on the pillow next to hers. Leaning over her bed, I was babbling, "Sadie all I care is that you are alive. That is all that counts."

Sunlight was coming in through the east window, while noises of far off traffic seeped in through the brick and glass enclosure.

Her father had to fly back to take care of the ranches. Her mother and I kept a twenty-four hour watch on her. She never wanted for water or food. There was not a body function she could take care of by herself. She was a complete invalid except for the movement in her right hand.

We received our diplomas in absentia with highest honors. There was a daily correspondence from Eastern. They were the kind of people who made sure all expenses were taken care of and that we were comfortable. There was enough insurance from the coliseum people to take care of us.

Eastern students had raised thirty thousand dollars to be put in a trust fund for future needs. Our college days were over, but our lives were not.

It was in July that Sadie's doctor thought it was best to transfer her to a rehabilitation facility for intensive therapy. "Young lady," he said, "you might not think you are good for much, but we are going to help you develop every talent possible. College authorities have informed me that you are an excellent writer. Perhaps you can develop in that line. As long as you live, you have to earn your keep."

Bill North from Bulton had been in touch with me. I had gone over twice and preached trial sermons when the board of deacons called and asked me to drive over and speak with them.

Bill carried the ball. "Hank, we are cattle people here. Our university people are very oriented towards the type of thing you are doing with rodeos. We think you can draw people in here with your type of sermon. We are willing to let you attend seminary and carry on speaking engagements. We even encourage you to carry on some rodeo activities. We expect you to be here twice on Sunday for your speaking engagements."

"What about Sadie?"

"We are glad you brought that up. We will expect nothing from her at all. You do plan to marry?"

"Certainly. First of August. She has already produced two short stories," I told them.

"We have had builders in fixing the house for her use. The Rehab Center has been most helpful. They say she will never be able to move around by herself. We think what we planned will please both of you."

I preached four Sundays in Bulton before Sadie came home for good. It was everything the deacons had hoped for. People flew in to the small airport east of town for my first morning service. Ranch and oil people from as far as Oklahoma City came. We ended up having two sermons so everyone could hear me. It was a heady experience.

My first sermon was simple. "How to keep in the saddle," was the message. My training in Eastern's humanities department had taught me that man is capable of doing a great deal for himself. My training in the Baptist Chair of Religion had taught me that some great men and women through the centuries had thought they were helped to keep in the saddle through faith in a Divine Being mirrored in Jesus Christ. I told it in cowboy language, which was easy to understand.

We had simple gospel singing of the country western type, a little above the Nashville popular music that Sadie liked so much.

It took five deacons working all afternoon to count the collection. I mention that first, but most important to me was that some young people seemed to make decisions that would be meaningful throughout their lives. And some old crusty types came forward with tears running down their cheeks and confessed crimes that would have put them in federal and state pens. You understand why I am not mentioning names.

You should know that I am still a non-believer. It was by accident I stumbled into religious speaking. There was a great deal of good done through my work. When it comes down to actually believing all that stuff they taught us in church history, about Jesus founding the Baptist Church when John the Baptist baptized him in the Jordan, I say, "Hog wash." Nor do I believe that Jesus meant to give Apostle Peter special privileges when he gave him the keys to the kingdom.

I built my theology on New Mexico's buttes and plains, with a whole lot of western mountains thrown in for support. My theology came out of a winter sky instead of stuffy books in schools that wanted to do nothing but argue about the correctness of their brand of theology.

Our first Sunday evening together was a time of sharing God's blessings. Never did my sermons try to convince, they only tried to strengthen. Never was I a hypocrite in my disbelief.

Sadie and I talked about going back to Nara Visa for the wedding. Her therapist, a large lady, sometimes blunt, but always truthful, said, "Sadie, your doctor and I have discussed this thoroughly. We both doubt that you are strong enough to be hassled around for any kind of big wedding. Also, both of you should know that there are certain injuries that are so life threatening that you will probably never be able to have any kind of normal sexual activities. It is up to you, Hank, if you want to try, but in all probability you will kill your wife."

Sadie was crying softly. It was nothing new to me, this announcement. There was no use brooding about it. Fortunately, there had never been a completion of the sexual act, so I had no idea of what there was to it. Very few of you will believe me, but it is true.

Sadie and I talked about it in the remaining week. We decided to cancel our plans, which we had been working on for a year. We planned a small wedding with only my mother and Sadie's parents present.

"Hank," she told me that evening, "you are getting a bad bargain. Sure you do not want to back out?"

"Sadie," I answered truthfully, "I would not know how to act around another woman. You have kind of trained me."

"What is there in it for you, Hank?" she asked.

"Your presence for one thing. Love is more than physical, something like looking at a sunset from the mesa. It is the feeling two people have when they love each other. We can learn to share things together. We have something that is deeper than most couples ever experience. I see New Mexico's strength in your face and hands. You have the blossom of yucca blossoms and prickly pear blooms in spring. All that which is beautiful is in you."

"Hank, if you ever find a woman who can give you physical love, take it. I will rejoice for you. Do not leave me. I shan't keep you long. You know the doctors have told me my body will degenerate rapidly, and I will not live more than five or six years."

"You will probably live to be a hundred, and I will enjoy every moment of it."

"Have you found someone to take care of me?"

"There is a Mexican woman in Bulton who has two little daughters to raise. She will stay day and night when I am away."

"Her name?"

"Carmelita."

"Wetback?" Sadie asked.

"Best that neither of us ever knows. She is learning English quickly. One thing about it, they built that parsonage to take care of a family of twelve."

"Do you like Bulton?" she asked.

"About as well as I did Portales. Same kind of people. They

strain at gnats and swallow camels. There are young minds at that university who can be shaped. Yes, I like it fine."

We had a beautiful wedding. My mother and Sadie's decorated the room with New Mexico plants that were not too showy in August's heat. They flew in sunflowers and Indian paintbrush blossoms, and plants that bloomed around the creeks and water holes. You would be surprised at what can be done with semi-desert plants.

Our major Bible professor from Eastern flew in and performed the service. He talked to me a long time before the service. "Hank," he started out, "you have chosen a hard row to hoe, and your friends at Eastern are proud of you. Try not to let your unbelief spread out to those who come to hear you. I studied you for three years intently. Frankly, I do not think your theology is any higher than some redskin riding round on a painted horse looking for buffalo."

"There were a number of them over our ranch for centuries. Most have been gone for years. Dad remembered Comanches riding across," I told him without batting an eyelash. We parted after the wedding with a strong handshake.

Sadie's mother stayed and helped us move into our new home. An ambulance service in Bulton came over and carefully moved Sadie. She had a back room which looked out over a well-kept lawn. The only way she moved all the time we were together was when she used her right hand to press buttons which allowed her to sit up and lie down. She had some simple exercises she performed daily. I loved her more than I did when we drove around in my old blue Dodge pickup.

She spent hours each day writing. First it was poetry about the mountains of Colorado, where we had spent that wonderful day. She wrote about the desert and had it published in some literary magazine. In three weeks she produced a major novel about the primitive people of New Mexico. It was a touching approach about a brave and his girlfriend, who lived together for five years in total isolation after their tribe banished both of them for breaking a tribal taboo of helping a senile old man left out to die.

Her first novel made the best selling list for two months straight.

Hollywood made it into a movie by Christmas.

There were weeks when we did little but speak occasionally. I always tried to spend Sunday afternoons with her. Four days a week, I drove to Fort Worth for school. It was a beautiful drive through rough ranch country a little more hilly than our New Mexico ranch land. There was Brazos River country, and a little black land, which had scattered cotton patches. Never did I tire of it.

Seminary was different from Eastern for the first two years. Professors lectured, and we listened. Most of them were inspiring. The church ran this school with an iron hand. Any professor who dared break the mold of the Southern Baptist Convention was severely disciplined. It was teach church dogma and forget about the multitude of questions that our eager minds raised.

Trustees emphasized it was Baptist money that was being used. They did not want a bunch of atheists being produced who even thought about checking the validity of the Bible, or of church dogma. I took to going and using Fort Worth's fine city library for more liberal writers. My grades for five years were straight A. Never did I question. Like a parrot, I learned to mouth back what often did not strike me as being true.

Once, a free thinker crept in for one semester, lasting for only five lectures. He let us question. He went on to a more liberal school back east, where he is now head of his department.

It was in Psychology of Religion classes that the professor gave stimulation that kept my intellect alive. We read some material by Dr. Wayne Oates, which allowed that even Baptists had anxiety and stress about their religion. Somehow our professor was able to bring in some Frued and Jung along with Hiltner and Brunner. Not enough to contaminate us with European thinking, but enough to make us wonder if there was not another world outside of Southwestern Baptist molded theology. It was dangerous stuff.

This is enough, but they brainwashed us. We came out studying and believing Church history based on deliberate falsification of ancient documents to prove the Baptist doctrine. Recent authors had changed "P's" to "B's" so that they could trace Baptist back to the time of John the Baptist by making Papist into Baptist.

You will say I wrote this because I am bitter about what happened. Sometime, if you are so inclined, take a Baptist history such as the Trail of Blood and trace it back to its historical source. You will find some interesting things, but it will take you more than an afternoon.

We raised over a million dollars in Bulton before Christmas for a new building. It was a magnificent structure with a central spire. The builder built the auditorium in such a way that the ushers seated people so they felt they were a part of the sermon. I was very proud of its simplicity. Still, we did not have room for our overflow crowds.

There were financial gains for the community, one of which was a steak house by the airport. People flew in from all over and ate before and after coming to church services. Local ranchers sold their meat direct for slaughter. For a flat fee, the owner furnished all the meat a family could eat at one meal.

Motels enlarged for the overflow crowds. Even the state school more than doubled its enrollment in two years. Their football games drew a full stadium. People took to coming and staying over for the Sunday service.

With all this, I rode the rodeo circuit. Only this time, I rode only in the bull riding. A church member flew me back and forth to major events. The deacons asked me to do this to keep my name in the headlines.

People started coming into town to buy new cars and pickups. It was amazing how my church helped the economy.

My only times of spiritual renewal were when Sadie and I visited three or four hours a week. She was the uncluttered place where I sought for human dignity without a lot of farce. She kept fat from developing between my ears. Some of you may understand.

In my Spartan life, I was like a Catholic priest pledged to celibacy. Very seldom did it bother me. There was a purity that shone forth from Sadie that melted all dross from my soul.

Her second novel was even more of a success than her first. It was about a bull rider who found an inner peace in the turmoil of the arena. It was not about me, but she did not know it.

She could turn on by looking at asters blooming with mums in the fall. That winter, ice storms burdened trees to breaking. There was a beauty she had never seen before. She showed me squirrels jumping from limb to limb. They occasionally fell from great heights. Never did it seem to hurt anything more than their pride.

She showed me beauty in red-capped woodpeckers and scarlet cardinals pecking on sunflower seeds. Occasionally, some real rare bird would fly in to her feeding station, which Carmelita and her girls kept well stocked.

"I do not know what I would do without you, Sadie."

"What do you mean, Hank? I do not understand."

"You have refined a complex life into a simple life full of meaning. From this bed, you have found out that life exists more in the soul than it does in the complex world. Somehow you have tapped in on the eternal. I have not been able to do it except through you."

"You mean you charge your battery here?" she asked.

"That is a simple way of putting it."

"Hank, I am glad you find something in me. You have given me so much."

Now you might realize that I was not sorry I married an invalid.

CHAPTER
SIX

During Christmas holidays at Southwestern, Sadie's mother came to relieve me. "Hank you deserve time off for good behavior. Go on home and relax for a few days. Your mother needs you."

The drive across northwest Texas's lonely landscape seemed to clear cobwebs out of my brain. There were snow flurries outside of Amarillo. Ice formed on my windshield thirty miles from Nara Visa.

No one knew about my arrival. When I entered Nara Visa from the east, nostalgia swept over me. Was what had happened to me really worth leaving this haven? Dad and his dad had grown up here without leaving. Their world had been narrow. Still, they had existed on New Mexico's plains without turning into monsters. After what had happened, breaking out of the shell seemed too painful.

Sadie's father let me know almost immediately that he thought what had happened to Sadie was, in part, my fault. "Hank, to be frank with you, that bull never would have hurt her if it had not been for you. Sadie would have been content to marry and stay here like her mother and your mother did."

"Dad, I gave her the choice."

"She wanted to please you."

"Anything I can do around here?"

"Your mother leased this place to me; you would only upset the help if you interfered." He was almost like I had deliberately caused his daughter to become crippled.

Different people react in different ways to tragedy. Should you want to know a person's true personality, watch him during a time of hardship and not a time of prosperity. He had been one who cheered us on the loudest when we were winning.

Mother had little time for me. She had developed a routine since Dad's death - a routine she did not like to break.

That afternoon, gathering up greyhounds in a trailer with a kennel, I went looking for coyotes. As I drove over pasture land, stray coyotes would come bounding out of draws. They would run out of rifle range and stand looking challengingly at me with tongues hanging out. We had tried several means of exterminating this vermin, but nothing worked except dogs.

I got as close as possible before releasing the hounds. They bounded out of the steel doors. Like convicts freed, they ran at full speed across the grassland. Never did they falter in their chase of the elusive coyote.

They caught the old coyote completely by surprise. While I watched from my knoll, a pack of hounds leveled out with the ground, racing towards their objective.

Too late, the coyote realized it had tarried longer than it should. Twelve hounds hit him at once. Fur flew. Gnashing teeth tore into tender hide. Out of the melee emerged the scarred hounds with nothing but a mangled carcass.

We stirred up three coyotes that afternoon under a leaden sky, which promised snow before morning. They hurt only one hound bad enough that it had a problem walking back to the cage.

It was while riding over this land so familiar, but still, after almost five years, so strange, that Sadie's absence fully hit me. She had walked over the bunchgrass with me. It was with her eyes I saw geese fly up from man-built tanks of water. She helped me see the beauty of a lonely windmill stark against the winter sky.

From one knoll, there were thirty of our cattle visible in the distance. Sadie always tried to guess the number without counting. It had been a game to see how close we could come.

Strange, I had not missed trying to reach a sexual climax with her until now. It swept over me how much I missed having her vibrant body against mine. So strong was the loss, it tore into me like a dull knife. Her face floated before me in the clouds, and I saw her shadow on the wind that raced across the cold prairie. It was the only time I ever cried. That day just before dark, I put my head on the old blue Dodge, which had meant so much to me, and cried until there were no more tears left.

There was nothing left for me in my beloved country. A stronger Being had seized my soul. At times during school, I had put myself to sleep remembering these familiar scenes. They were still here, but I was not. All across the western sky there was a blaze of color, where the dying sun sent rays into its foes, the clouds.

There was still an unrest in my soul that fought against preaching a Gospel that had no relevance for me most of the time. There had never been a strong guilt built up in me. Never had I really come to religion for a cleansing like some had done.

One of the old English saints had felt he was walking in blood every time he came to a sinful English town. What people did and felt had no meaning to me, unless it threatened my way of life.

There was a thin layer of ice on our front window through which shone bright lights Mother had used to decorate her lonely tree. She never mentioned it, but I knew she missed Dad terribly. With me she had seen that my life had turned away from the ranch and what it meant.

"Guess I'll head back in the morning, Mother."

"Must you leave so soon, Hank?"

"Hate to leave Sadie too long this close to Christmas. She tries not to, but it gets lonely for her. It seems she misses up here more than I do."

"Don't you think about home anymore, Hank?"

"Time goes fast when there is much to do, Mother. Some days there are not enough hours in the day. Two foreign languages this semester has kept me hopping."

"Foreign languages?"

"Greek and Hebrew."

"Both of them at one time?" she asked.

"Greek, I am proficient with. Hebrew, I need before taking too many Old Testament courses."

"Are you happy, Hank?"

"My lot in life seems pretty well cut out for me. Religion was not my big concern."

"Why did you ever choose it?"

"It was something I was good at doing. It meant something to Sadie."

"She has been a big influence on you, hasn't she?"

"We are inseparable."

"You never made love to her, did you?"

"No, Mother, nor will I ever."

"Some women are like that, Son. They always manage to stay out of a man's reach. When you two were growing up, I watched you. Sadie always stayed just out of your going through with a sexual act. Sometimes I wanted to tell you not to let her do you that way, but my motherly instincts always got in my way. It isn't reasonable for a mother to tell her son wrong things to do."

"It was not any more Sadie's choice than it was mine."

"Son, a woman always controls those things. A man thinks he chooses the kind of sex life he is going to have, but a woman does the rest. One of these days you are going to meet a woman who will turn you on. You will blame yourself for what will happen. It won't be anymore your fault than it is Sadie's. Come and talk it over with me if I am still alive."

"Thank you, Mother. I am handling things pretty well so far."

"Always have been that way, Hank, every since you were a baby. What has come over me? You are starved."

"I will admit I can eat."

She dished out steaks and potatoes with gravy. Out of a full pot, she dished up a bowl of turnip greens.

"My favorite meal."

"I remember. Your name's been in the paper a lot. Your daddy was real proud of you. Tell me something about your studies. Don't reckon I really talked to a preacher real seriously."

We sat at the table covered with a gleaming white tablecloth. It was not placed there for me, it was the way she lived. A delicate blue lampshade cast a shadow across the attractive meal.

"Missed your cooking. Some of seminary is interesting. I really enjoy archaeology and Old Testament studies. Only thing is, it strikes me once in a while that the Hebrews must not have been much more religious than our American Indians."

"What do you mean?" Mother asked.

"Both of them seem to believe they communed with a Spirit who told them what to do."

"Indians were so cruel, Son. How can you make a comparison?"

"Read about the way Hebrews treated their enemies. Mutilated them sexually. Killed them when they had already surrendered. Things like that."

"God told them to do it so they could have a land free of idol worshippers," Mother said.

"Maybe Indians felt that way. Are we sure Plains Indians were not trying to clear out idol-worshipping Aztecs? We do not know what their purpose in life was."

"Seemed kind of pointless to me."

"It might seem some of the things we do are that way to foreigners."

"Never thought of it that way. You learn that in seminary?"

"They would dismiss me as a heretic if I even discussed it. There is not any freedom of religion behind those closed doors. Trouble with going to a state university, a person learns to question too many things. Sometimes it seems like they try to favor those Baylor graduates even over some of those small Baptist schools in Texas," I told Mother.

"You lost me. All I ever knew about religion was from reading my Bible and praying. Seemed what preachers preached contradicted what they did so much, I never really listened. God always talked to me out here when I was by myself."

"Still feel that way, Mother. Organized religion is a farce, like politics. It is fun to play around with."

"Do not get burnt. Tell Sadie I enjoyed her book. Admire the way she is making something out of herself. Must be hard on you."

"You are the only person who has ever said that. People seldom think about the other person when there is one who gets hurt. It gets depressing at times, but I am too busy to let it bother me."

"Best you keep that way. Sorry to see you go so soon. How does the land look this year?"

"Best I ever saw it. Sadie's father keeps the place well."

"I get half the money made on this place. That is more than when your daddy was running it. Seems like added responsibility has remade Sadie's father. He used to be haphazard. He is wonderful to me. Ever regret you did not come back and run the ranch?"

"Every day," I said.

"You are young, you may come back."

"Doubt it."

"Things happen that change a person's mind."

Next morning, there was a foot of snow over everything from horizon to horizon. While we slept, a new stage prop dropped down while the curtain closed. It was that way for me, a new scene came in my life.

I drove back through a white wasteland which stretched from Nara Visa to Wichita Falls. After that, it was cold all the rest of the way into Fort Worth.

Bill came over soon as I had a chance to unload the car. "Hank, some of our people are awful upset you have not had anything to say about those dances they are holding out at the university. They want you to act against it."

"Danced all the time I was in school. What do they have against it?"

"Seems it causes too many pregnancies. They found whiskey bottles behind the gym."

"Found a whiskey bottle behind the church building last week after church," I said.

"Must have been a bum did it."

"Could have been a bum out at the university."

"Some of those kids are pretty wild."

"Bill, I do not like drinking, but dancing is different. Seems like instead of trying to close things down, we should be trying to change people so they do not do wrong."

"I am telling you what the deacons sent me over to tell you.

Either you start trying to change things round here, or we will look for another preacher who will." Bill shouted his warning.

"Is that you speaking?"

"No. The other deacons told me to speak to you in that tone. Frankly, you have done more for this church than any other preacher ever has. It's made a difference in my life, the approach you have. I do not really think anyone will let you go."

"Tell them they came looking for me. I can make more rodeoing than I can here. I'll preach against intemperance in any phase of life, but whether a college student dances or not is his own business."

"How about Sadie? You thought about her?" Bill asked.

"Two of us together have one hundred sections of land we can make a living from. Her novel has brought in twice as much as I made here. Besides, an oil company wants my name on their letterhead. They are offering a hundred thousand. Tell your people not to threaten me again."

It worked. Next Sunday, the deacons met me with big smiles on their faces. "Happy to see you, Hank. Finest sermon you ever preached. Is there anything we can do for you?"

It was my ball game. I never looked in their eyes.

There was a professor in charge of one of the humanities departments who kept me going. Tall, he looked like a long gangling bird when he walked. His main pleasure in life was to make life difficult for me. I met him every time I went to the post office.

I can still see the grin on his face when he approached me with an argument about why religion was a bastard from some primitive urge for man to cleanse a primeval sex guilt from his soul. We crossed swords. Little did he know I agreed with him most of the time.

Only time his points did not touch me was after a young person had lost control and turned his or her life around after coming forward at a Sunday service. One day I told him, "Professor, the subject you teach has added a great deal of pleasure to my life. I even gained more insights on life in an English classroom than I did in a religion class. Only thing is, reading Shakespere has never turned a person completely around and pointed them in another direction."

He harumphed amd cleared his throat. "Maybe you were not aware of the change."

A light came into his eyes. "Have you ever seen Shakespeare make a man so miserable he would jump off a ten story building? Religion does that sometimes."

He had me, and I knew it. The only thing I could say was, "Some English professors go insane."

"So do preachers," he countered. We parted to build ammunition. He kept me on my toes better than that back-biting board of deacons.

We had some seminary professors who were real different. One started off his lecture after Christmas with a tale drug through many a preacher's convention. "Christmas made me think of this one," he said. "There was a preacher who had to leave a church over a hot issue. He was an old man ready to retire. `Watch me when I walk down the aisle. There is a message for you all.' Anxiously, the members turned their heads to watch him walk. All who could see observed that he had a sprig of mistletoe tied to his coattail."

After we finished laughing, he said, "Each one of you will feel like doing that sometime or other in your ministry. Hank, you are the only one I ever heard of having a church after doing it. Congratulations."

There were more icy road that winter than I had ever seen before. It was impossible to get home three or more times. One dreary afternoon, when I was looking for a free place to throw my sleeping bag, a familiar figure loomed up before me. It was Kent, my roommate. He was not preacher material when we were in school.

"Kent," I called. "What are you doing here?"

"Decided if you could make a living and stay out of the draft here, I could also."

We shook each other's hands until we almost shook them off.

"Where you staying?" I asked.

"Batching it in the men's dorm."

"Place I can throw my sleeping bag down?"

"Like old times. Come on and let's catch up on things. How is married life?"

"Fine. You heard about Sadie?" I asked.

"All they talked about the last week of school. Fine thing you did going through with the marriage."

"Other way around, Kent. It was a fine thing she married me."

"If your sermons are half as good as her novel, they are good."

"People fly in from all over to hear me."

"Heard that. Regular cow-pasture preacher. Let's get out of this cold."

It was way after midnight before we slept. "You know, Hank, guess every person feels his school was best after he graduates. Eastern was really unique. Seems like they were able to make us do some thinking while we enjoyed it." I agreed.

Kent was a regular visitor to our home. Sadie's face lit up every time he walked through the door.

That Saturday, I rode the bulls at Amarillo. It was my greatest outlet, sitting on that animal and letting both of us take our frustrations out. One I drew bucked and pitched. He tried to wear me out. It was while I was doing everything to keep my hat on that one of my greatest religious experiences hit me. It was not exactly an audible voice, but sure as Saul heard a voice on his way to Damascus, I did also. "Hank, you are trying to ride life like it is a bull. Let up and enjoy it. Stop fighting everything."

Things lightened up after that. Once again there was a world with trees and bushes. There was even a little time to stop and catch a catfish on the Brazos. Once I came in wet and muddy after spending the afternoon chasing stray heifers which crawled through a barbwire fence.

I noticed flocks of blackbirds swirling through the winter sky. It marveled me how they never hit. I have been to a lot of places, but Central Texas, in the old maize fields up and down the Brazos, is the only place where blackbirds perform such group aerial feats.

"Hank," Sadie said, "I am glad you got a devil off your back before it destroyed you. Welcome home."

I kissed her tenderly before washing the mud down the driveway. Things went easier after that.

Next time I saw the professor, I won my point. His face lit up. "See you found yourself. Do it in that dull Bible of yours?"

"No, in a maize field over on the Brazos."

"Found a bit of myself along some of these Texas streams myself."

It was the first time we departed friendly, without crossing swords.

CHAPTER
SEVEN

In June, Bulton Church sent me to Louisville for the Southern Baptist Convention. Baptists teach that our country's government was patterned after their type of government. Messengers go to state and national conventions to elect officials and make policies for the vast body of believers. Presbyterians claim the distinction of founding democracy where delegates govern even the local church.

It is my opinion that each denomination contributed its share towards our national government, along with other congregational churches, who put their two cents in, too.

Kentucky, in early summer, was a flower bed. Grass does not grow on top of dry mesas in New Mexico. Here, a luxurious growth covered all bare land. There were tall trees surrounded by bushes and flowers, some of which I never saw before.

It will not be necessary to bore you with details of this sprawled out meeting, which took over Kentucky's state fairground. There is no meeting, unless it is a bunch of Elks, who are ruder and noisier than the people at the Southern Baptist Convention.

Old classmates of southern schools spend this time visiting. If a person wants to hear various speakers, they have to sit in front row seats to hear above the uproar.

There have been three distinct groups in the convention for several years. At the top of the hierarchy are those liberals who have studied at Yale, Princeton, Harvard and Southern state universities. They emerged with a humanitarian education and a Biblical view that uses every tool in a modern scientific world to search out the truth of Biblical study. People in this group are apt to take a toddy before bedtime. The other two groups look on this group as less than Christian.

Next in line are Conservative Baptists who uphold Baptist beliefs, but who tend to take a more scientific approach to Biblical studies. This group is inclined to say that they do not know how the world was created, only that God had a hand in its beginning and continuation.

At bedrock are those called Fundamentalists. This group believes in a literal interpretation of the King James Version of the Bible. God created the world in six, twenty-four hour days and on the seventh he rested. For them, the Baptist religion started with Christ's baptism, and there has been a continuous, unbroken passing on of the fire since that time.

I am sorry to bore you, but this book is placed in such an atmosphere. You have to understand this to understand some of the things that happened to me.

The outcome of the convention was they chose me to chair a committee on the best ways to evangelize western ranch people. My group was a sub-committee of a sub-committee, but for one my age, it was an honor. It was like a lawyer being elected to a committee on the state legislation while still in the first year of law school.

It was a hot Texas summer that greeted me when the plane came down at Love Field. After the more moderate Kentucky climate, it knocked me for a spell.

Summer doldrums had hit the Bulton church. You may wonder about the town's name. Some would swear early settlers gave it the name because of the amount of bull spread around by old men sitting on the courthouse steps whittling.

A county seat, it received its name from Colonel F. A. Bulton, who led a charge of Confederate soldiers at Bull Run. It is a town located in a valley with rolling hills on the east and west. Bisecting through the town is a small river, which has been harnessed with government conservation dams.

Some of its more rural areas are mostly wilderness, with large oak and pecan trees. Troublesome mesquite trees took over most of its productive cotton land. Perhaps this is God's way of protecting barren soil, by causing a less favorable tree, bush or weed to protect exposed soil.

The land was not as isolated as my country in Nara Visa, but it had its beauty. It took me more than a year to get used to its closed-in wooded groves of trees that kept me from seeing farther than across the street.

My first night home, I had a local restaurant cater a real Texas barbequed rib meal for Sadie and me. Rosita was instructed to fix us an eating place with a white tablecloth and our best silverware and china.

Barbecue is not often thought proper for such a meal. It was our kind of food.

"I have missed you, Hank."

"Also, Sadie."

"Tell me about what you saw and heard."

"There were some great speeches. It worries me that there seems to be a strong breech in beliefs in our Convention. Should it grow worse, it might cause a schism in our great denomination. Let me help you with that meat."

"Thank you, Hank. I hate to hear that."

"Church policy has always interested you more than it has me. Still, it seems that this will eventually break up the unity of our work. Maybe two Conventions will grow more rapidly into two large works. We will have to wait and see," I told her.

"Hank, it seems that it has been the South's fate to fight among itself. Guess we missed that part of our heritage in New Mexico."

"Always wondered if it isn't this God-awful heat that makes us fight the way we do."

"What are your plans for the summer?" Sadie asked.

"My work with the Convention will take some time."

"What work is that?"

"Forgot to tell you, they chose me to head up a committee on evangelizing western ranch people."

"What an honor for one so young, Hank! If anyone knows anything about the subject, you should."

"My work here was the reason they chose me. There is no use

trying to pull ranch hands in to hear some of these highfalutin' sermons and music. Amazing Grace sung by a choir dressed in western clothes can be every bit as sacred as the music in some of these big city churches."

"I liked some of the more classical things also, Hank."

"Me too, but it is not what we like, it's what will draw people."

"Are you attending class this summer?" Sadie asked.

"Best one. It is a seminar conducted by the psychology department on a study of what happens in the human mind when there is a religious experience."

"How can you test something that personal?"

"I have been chosen to draw up a test that will objectively measure the change in human personality after what we call the conversion experience."

"How interesting. What kind of test are you planning on using?"

"Open ended questions, multiple choice. We are going to determine if conversion modified a select group of people's behavior significantly."

"How interesting. What areas are you going to examine?"

"Hobbies, reading, sexual feelings, temper and some other areas of the personality. We have a clinical psychiatrist working with us."

"Do you think you can find what area of the human brain the religious conversion affects?"

"Perhaps. Some in the medical profession would say the religious conversion does more harm than good."

"From what we studied at Eastern, Hank, it would seem that the long range effects of most mood altering drugs used on mental wards have been devastating on the psyche."

"It has always been that way. One school of thought thinks religion is only a placebo, others think it is a vital part of our society."

"Aren't you going to have any time for yourself?"

"Thought I might go surf fishing for a few days on the coast. One of the deacons is lending me his motor home."

"Too bad you cannot buy one for yourself."

"It would be a waste until I get out of school."

"Any rodeoing?"

"Cheyenne is all. Just enough to keep me in the circuit. My name draws people from all over the west. Church wants me to reach out into summer retreats and such this summer."

"You must be awfully tired, Hank."

"Not really. Only thing I miss is having you with me. It would be such a pleasure for you to see the things I'm seeing."

"Your reports are all I need."

"What are your plans for your next novel?"

"I'm going back to Middle Eastern culture and do one on the life and times of Christ when he was a boy."

"Interesting. Think you can get enough material?"

"I will use my imagination."

I left for the coast after evening church services. It was a long drive on narrow roads, until at last I reached the vast expanse of Texas's magnificent bays and waterways before daylight. It was a totally new world for me. There were the sounds of feeding water birds, while fish splashed in the ever-rolling surf.

My plans were to hit the beach at Port LaVaca, fish a spell, drive, and fish some more until I reached my destination at Port Isabella. The upper end of Padre Island was all the farther I got.

Driving down this wide expanse of sand by the Gulf's sparkling blue water was awe-inspiring for a drylander from New Mexico. First day there, my cast brought a sudden jerk followed by a singing reel. I landed a small shark. It was the downfall for my plans.

I spent nights around a roaring fire built out of driftwood found on the sand. Avoiding all people, it was a much needed retreat from my hectic schedule.

This was a time of inward reflection. I tried to reconcile my beliefs with my actions. It seemed that professional counseling was going to be needed to help me keep on an even emotional keel with problems caused by Sadie's physical condition.

My mind was willing, but my flesh was not totally subdued. My restless sex drive caused me concern. It was not enough that I tried to rationalize that men in isolated parts of the world led lives of celibacy. I was not in isolation, nor was I sworn to celibacy by a religious vow.

My mother's comments caused me some concern. Was it possible that I would break my marriage vows and go to another woman for sexual fulfillment?

This trap caught too many of my preacher friends. Their reputations ruined, they constantly shifted jobs, trying to run away from their unsavory reputations. It was not easy in the Baptist denomination to have a private life. Constantly there would be a member, even in the most isolated area, who would be there to catch any erring behavior.

There are those who think ministers are snoops, always trying to seek out sins of their parishioners. From my observations, it was equally as true that a church member would try to find flaws in the minister's personal life.

The second night lessened my morbid thinking centered on rodeos and religion. Morning light revealed strange markings in the sand unmarked by human footprints. A new physical environment brought out my curiosity. Like a small child, I started digging holes in the sand to find out what creatures along the water's edge caused slight bubbles in the shallow surf.

There were strange crabs, which borrowed other creature's shells to carry 'round like a borrowed house, much like a renter would rent a house. Along the sandy beaches, fiddler crabs ran their odd patterns when they scurried before me, like a piece of flotsam blown upon the lonely sand.

That afternoon, I hiked across sand dunes and marsh grass to where an inland sea washed between permanent land and the ever-shifting sand dunes, where I parked the mobile home.

There was a fascinating land here in this lonely place, where only sea gulls scolded me when I waded out into a pounding surf and cast my cut bait of squid and mullet.

It was drawing towards mid-afternoon when my surf casting equipment almost tore out of my gloved hand. A hundred pound test line stripped off while I used my heavy glove to stop the smoking reel. Setting the brake, my reel sang when it tried to slow down this creature of the deep, which ran with a hook in his gut.

It was way after sundown before it came up into shallow surf and then turned back into the lonely sea. Once again, its force made me follow its pull, lest it tear my equipment from my hand.

My legs grew weary, while I kept constant pressure against the angled rod. There were times I thought of cutting the line and letting the retching, tearing fish go back into its habitat of salt water.

There was an early moon that cast a velvet haze over the whole sea coast. Its beams danced on rippling waves like fairy feet on lily pads.

Far out in the Gulf, lights shone from off-shore drilling rigs that bored holes down through the ocean floor into a primeval layer of compressed gas and oil. There was little time for thinking, until the giant fish once again turned and came shoreward.

This time, with a constant pressure on the line, it was possible to beach this giant of the deep. From all my calculations of heaving its struggling body, it must have weighed a good seventy pounds.

Voices spoke in the darkness, startling me. "Señor, how much for fish?"

"No use to me. You eat him?"

There was a Mexican man with two small boys and a girl. "Sí Señor, we eat much fish. Bring him to light so we can see what kind he is."

Dragging the fish around to where we could turn the Mexican's headlights on my fish, he instantly recognized it as a drum. "Muy bueno, Señor. It will feed my family for a week."

Struggling, we loaded the fish on his makeshift sand buggy, which he drove proudly towards the lights away in the distance.

It was late when I woke to sunlight streaming in my window. Hungry gulls followed schools of fish up and down the beach. They swooped and rose with finney creatures in their beaks. After breakfast, I found that gulls would come in fast if I threw bread slices in the air. They swooped and fought with each other over these morsels.

Since it was Saturday, I made my way northward towards a church that repelled and drew me. My faith in the God I preached was no stronger than it had been that first time in college, when I had given a ten minute account of riding an angry bull in the rodeo arena and compared it to life.

It was to be a pattern to my life. Preaching, a little rodeoing, school and an occasional fishing trip to the coast, or a shorter trip to large inland lakes.

That summer, I used part of my savings to buy my own pickup with a camper on it. There was no need for a car since Sadie could not ride anyway.

This became my home for short times away from the grind. Soon, my church members grew used to me taking off after Sunday night services for my one-night fishing trips. It was good I established this schedule in their minds.

Church was not my only responsibility that summer. My work with the denomination developed into cowboy revivals across four states. Under star-studded skies, western people met in isolated places to sing and listen to preaching.

Some came to see the champion all-'round cowboy. Others wanted to shake hands with the most talked about bull rider on the circuit, a rider and a preacher. Others, who were in the majority, came to listen and worship.

We had seminars in isolated rural areas for those wishing to get away from their busy schedules.

Many a night, coyotes tuning their chorus into a crescendo accompanied our cowboy choirs in their melodic tunes out on the lonesome plains.

Toward the end of August, my preaching took me up past Nara Visa for a night meeting in the mountains at Glorieta, where the Baptists had an encampment on a mountain side.

There was a rich oil man in Bulton who made one of his private planes and an experienced pilot available to fly me anywhere I needed to go in my duties. It would have been impossible to have driven over that large area during the five years until I finished seminary.

This time, the pilot brought our plane down on the morning-lit runway in my home town. Swooping down over the vast prairie was much different from driving down its lonely highway, trying to keep awake, while the treeless plain drifted the driver into a death-dealing sleep.

Mother met me and we had lunch together.

"Hank, it is so good to see you. I try and keep up with your traveling, but it seems you get around more than the President."

"Sometimes I wonder where I went, Mother. A few times I have not known where I was. It has been an interesting life, but where it is leading is a question."

"Son, the reason you got my letter asking you to stop by soon as you can is that Sadie's father has formed a cattle company with a large oil company. He wants to buy me out."

"How do you feel about it, Mother?"

"I can stay in the house, but Hank, I do not want our ranch getting out of our hands."

"Do you need the money?"

"No. Your father left me well off. There has been plenty of money coming off the land to live on without touching any of our capital."

"Hang on to this place, will you? There may be a time when I will need a place to come home."

"Sadie's father argues that with you two being only children all this will come to you anyway."

"Still rather we keep our part separate from his deal. Things can happen when a person starts dealing with a big company."

"All I wanted to hear, Son. How is Sadie?"

"About the same. She does not seem to get any better. Strange part about it, she cheers me up."

"She has been good for you, Hank. You would have been lost without her. It seems such a shame that a talented person like Sadie has to live like she does. It does not seem fair somehow."

"Why don't you drive me out home? We can talk on the way. Wish I could stay the night, but there is a meeting I have to attend at seven."

"It does not seem possible you could be back by then."

"Airplanes are wonderful inventions. Let me tell the pilot so he will not sit out in this hot sun all that time."

Once again, I renewed myself by driving the familiar straight road across the plains to home. Any minute I expected my father to step out and greet me. It would be such a pleasure to lean on his strong shoulder for a few minutes.

We brought a cloud of dust with us when the car made its steady journey over land that had not seen rain for more than a month.

"There going to be enough grass to carry cows this summer?"

"We need to sell off a bunch of steers, Son. Prices are good. Yes, there is plenty of feed and water. We have had such good years. It is about due for a bad one soon."

We did not stop at the house, but drove on past over the rolling prairie back down in the rougher cedar brake country.

I told my mother about the Gulf and its fascination for me.

"See any good-looking women down there, Son?"

"Was not looking, Mother."

"You are a strange one, Hank. Thought all men were looking for a woman. Your father was never gone overnight without straying a little. Do not know that he ever caught one, but he tried."

"Guess my work is taking the place of a woman. There is something about what I am doing that keeps me totally involved. I do not seem to have time for anything else."

"How is your psychology project coming?" Mother asked.

"That has been fascinating. There seem to be definite patterns of behavior showing up the more we study people. Those with a strong sexual drive seem to take a number of conversion experiences to keep them on the Christian journey. This fall we plan to find persons who were once very active in church and find out what caused them to check out."

"Think your work will ever amount to anything?"

"We have some behavioral people very interested. First major breakthrough of religion catching thoughts of professional medical people. With electronic computers with brains activated and directed by messages, we are beginning to wonder if the Christian conversion experience does not alter a command module in the brain."

"Interesting, Hank. Wonder if man will not get too smart for his own good one of these days."

"What I am interested in is finding a means of behavioral

modification other than chemicals, which will change a human from a destructive life into a productive one. State and federal prisons are filling up quicker than the states can build new ones."

"Think you could trust a murderer enough to turn him back into society after a conversion?"

"I do not know, Mother. There have been some wicked men turned into model citizens through religion. Only thing is it is impossible, without years of observation, to tell if a person had a genuine religious experience. I am sure no law enforcement official is going to be willing to parole a dangerous criminal without more proof than we have."

"The Bible says that a day is coming when God's word will be written on men's minds so that they will do good instead of bad. Maybe you can bring that time to pass."

"Swear, sometimes you amaze me, mother. You grasp things some of those seminary professors with doctor degrees do not."

"Son, some people who learned in the school of hard knocks know more than you educated people think we do. Your father and I used to talk about ways to alter people's minds so they would not go to war anymore. Your father was always much against fighting."

"Vietnam is a mess. Sometimes I feel pretty guilty about not going."

"Don't. You are doing more good here than you could ever do there. It seems the United States gets itself in the biggest messes sometimes."

"Hate to break this up, but I need to stop by and see Sadie's parents a moment. Her mother might want to fly back with me."

Mother turned the car around and we drove back across the way we had come. With all the new places I had seen, this was still my favorite. Sometimes I wished Sadie and I had settled down here in a big house like we had planned.

Every person I had ever spoken to who had a tragedy like ours thought the same thing. If only they had followed a different road or stayed in bed another hour, there would not have been the accident. It seemed one could not alter life enough to take care of those things.

Perhaps there was a divine blueprint that people followed. Were there marked routes that led to destruction? I did not know, but if I could have altered the route that led to Sadie's destruction, I would have done it. Only thing we might have come home and met with a worse accident.

Sadie's father never took this train of thought. We no sooner stopped at the house than he brought the subject around to how Sadie could have still been a normal person if we had only stayed here instead of going to school. He could make me feel guilty in minutes. There was no way to let him know how much I grieved over the situation.

"Your mother decide to sell?" he asked.

"I do not think so."

"I am not pushing her. Only thing, there is a chance we could really make this land produce with some capital behind us. The oil company will not go along with the deal unless you folks throw in."

"Land's been in the family for generations. Something about having land makes a person more of a person. I can stand on my own two feet, Dad. You take this land away from me, I will fall flatter than a flitter. Think I could tell that board of deacons where to head in without this place?"

He said, "Kind of your security blanket? Maybe it is best this way; I am not twisting your arm. You have room for both of us to fly back with you? Things are kind of slack right now, and I want to see Sadie if you can stand me."

"Sure can. She will be so thrilled. We have to be on our way. I have an appointment at seven."

"We better hump it. It is four now. There is no use your mother driving you into town. We will take my car and leave it at the airport and hitch a flight back."

It was a pattern that we developed. Whenever I could, I stopped by. It was a long dry spell that our two families had to ride out. If it had not been for high cattle prices, they might have gone under. That next summer, Sadie's dad thanked me for not selling. "Hank, those oil people would not have stuck with it like we did. They do not have the interest of the land at heart like your mother and me."

CHAPTER
EIGHT

Sometimes, when I look back at what happened, I must have cared about the church and what it stood for. Sadie would have been much more comfortable at home, looking out on our ranches, instead of lying looking out into a back yard in Bulton.

There was nothing holding me except my desire to make my church one of the largest in the state. My whole purpose in life was to be number one. Was not that my goal from the start? My psychiatrist friend I slipped off and went to that fall tried to make me see this.

"Hank, you bucked for first place all your life. It must have been something in your early childhood. Look at you. Best quarterback, best rodeoing, best speaker. Are you satisfied? No. You are pushing to have the biggest church in the state plus being a number one, all-American hero by marrying your wife and sacrificing your whole sex life."

"Anything wrong with that?" I asked.

"I forgot number one seminary student. How many hours have you spent on this research project I am monitoring? Your work is brilliant. No, there is nothing wrong in what you are doing, unless you cross a path you cannot handle. You will blow all to pieces if you step out of line one bit." He paused to study notes.

"You told me your mother thought Sadie was the type who kept men at a safe distance. She is safe; you cannot touch her, but there are other women. When you find that one, you will explode."

"What can I do about it?"

"Listen, I do not think there is any therapy program that will help you. All you can do is go ahead and when you blow up, come back here and let's see if we cannot put the pieces back together. In the meantime, take up hunting. A man aggressive as you are, needs a violent outlet."

There was little spare time. I bought me a deer rifle, if only to hang on my gun rack in the pickup. It looked good there, as did all the other guns carried around in Texas.

Kent and I went hunting three or four times on a deer lease one of my church members provided. There was a deer stand and all. Two of us climbed the ladder Thanksgiving day and watched the brush for a deer to appear.

Kent shot one first. It was a six point buck. It was nothing like the big mule deer Dad and I had hunted over west, close to Cuba. Kent took one look at this little deer and said, "One thing New Mexico has is bigger deer than Texas. Ought to make some meat. Let's skin it out and take it in. Chances are we will not see anything else today."

Rosita was prouder of that venison than she would have been of an elk. She must have made at least twenty dishes out of it. We had sausage, chili, ribs, steaks, you name it.

It was my turn to get one the next morning. My shot hit a nine point buck straight between his eyes. We climbed up in the blind well before dawn on a cold, frosty morning. It was after sunup before this deer came creeping out of the woods. He did not suspect a thing.

It was two days of therapy, and I did not feel one bit different because of my hunting.

Everything was going well at school and at church. Sadie was comfortable with her writing. It was time to relax and let things run themselves. One thing, that church never caused me to lose a night's sleep. It was a good paying job, but there were many other good paying jobs.

I did spend a great deal of time thinking up original and interesting sermons. This is another contradiction; the church did not mean anything to me, but I put a great deal of time into preparation.

The building was full almost every Sunday. We had three Sunday morning services plus the evening one. Like Catholics, we found there were hundreds of people who would stop by church at six o'clock Sunday morning before starting their day. Some wanted to hunt and fish, but others had family plans that took them out of town. The other extra service we started so we would not have to enlarge our auditorium.

The Southern Baptist Convention sent in experts to analyze what we were doing. While other churches were struggling along with half crowds and no money, we were drawing from at least a five-hundred mile radius and we had two television hook-ups for two services. Never did I have people put their hands on the television set while I prayed for them.

In fact, very few of my sermons were on healing as such. My messages centered around God and His love, not on His wrath. Somehow I was able to bring in the western breeze and the mountain air. Whiffs of pine smoke from blazing campfires mingled with stories from Palestine. Jesus rode a rodeo horse.

Do not think Bulton's people were without criticism, especially about my leaving Sadie so much while on my trips, for pleasure and work, which took me from home so much. Old ladies would have had me staying with her twenty-four hours a day, except Sunday services.

Bulton people were not the kind who merely thought. They were a cruel, malicious group of people who gossiped out loud in my presence.

Sarah Jennings was my most ardent supporter and my most severe critic. A tall, thin lady with bad breath, she would find me visiting with my friend Kent, and whisper in a voice that would carry all over the church. "Looks to me like he could stay home with his wife more. Church does not pay him to run all over the country. He goes to Fort Worth four days a week. Rodeos two days a month at least, then flies all over to those camp meetings he has going. Rest of the time he is off hunting or fishing with that friend of his from college."

It was always best to tune her out before she brought up the fact we might be gays carrying out our activities on some dark deer stand. Somehow, in those early years, my work took the place of all those sexual experiences that other men my age engaged in.

Sadie preferred having me come in her room and visit at odd times rather than be around the house all the time. "Hank, I would hate you if we had to live here together twenty-four hours a day. You would murder me, and if I could lay my hands on a pistol, you would be dead."

What you have to understand is that Sadie did not lie without something to do like some of the church people did. She had a typewriter for one-armed people with which she could type faster than some people with ten fingers.

Her third book was already on the press. It might not be as much of a moneymaker as the others, but at least it was going to make people think. She was not one to do everything for money. Some of her syndicated articles to newspapers attacked public figures by names when she thought they needed it.

Sadie was reading three major newspapers and one local paper a day. She limited television watching to two hours most days, but those two hours she spent watching current events, except for a worthwhile play or movie. She did not spend her time in idleness.

"Hank, if you want to do me a favor, get rid of these church people who want to come in and sit all day looking at me. If there is anything I hate, it's an old bitch sitting here with tears in her damn eyes looking at me like I am a poor lamb she has to cheer up."

It was not easy, and we lost friends, but I enforced her wishes. She had two or three friends who came in. I do not know what they discussed, but their high pitched conversations were followed by feminine laughter. It was always time for me to leave home when these parties started.

"I heard they are playing bridge over there in that parsonage," Sarah Jennings whispered in my presence one Sunday morning. "Looks like much as we are paying him, she could spend her time praying."

Her companion countered with, "She cannot play bridge, Sarah, she only has one hand."

"Rich like they are, no telling what they thought up so she can carry on her devilment. Never did think we should have called a preacher from a state school, they pick up all kinds of evil habits."

That Sunday, in middle of the service, my sermon turned from "God and the West" to "God and a Fiery Tongue." It stopped Sarah for one afternoon.

In the middle of the second year, the church hired Kent to help me. A stocky half German, half Cherokee, he was able to hold things together for me better than anyone else. He was quiet. No one in college would ever have thought of him developing into a public speaker. He developed his own style, which was much different from mine.

He was really good with young people. He held youth rallies at the university even when those in charge objected violently to bringing religious services on campus. With enough money and a few friends in the right places, we were able to do a lot of things that no one thought we could. Our main accomplishment was bringing in a group of Christian singers from Nashville and having a Grand Old Opry kind of thing in the football stadium.

I am for separation of state and church as much as the next person, but when a school can bring in a bunch of freaks with their hair dyed purple and green, then it is time to change the pattern. Besides, most country western music is built on our Christian heritage. Even honky-tonk music emphasizes the concept of Puritan good and evil.

My friend from the English Department belabored this point a few times in a voice high enough for the town people to walk clear out in the parking lot to avoid us.

"Hank," he said, "you are using state property to advance the Baptist Churches' narrow views."

"Did you ever hear me mention the Baptist Church on state property?"

"No," he said with a puzzled frown, which I came to recognize as a sign he was thinking, "but you are trying to modify these students' minds with your Christian thinking."

"Aren't you trying to fill their minds with a Godless humanistic doctrine without any point or meaning?"

We were yelling. "My department is trying to make people face reality. You money-sucking preachers try to suppress all of a student's emotions into your ecclesiastical machinery, which takes the worth of the individual and turns it into a grape juice to serve in communion on Sunday morning. Your church draws people in, brainwashes them, and spits out the dredges like a giant catsup-making machine. You want to make everyone into a stereotyped reprint of the original."

"Like Jesus?"

"Hank, not like Jesus. Like what you think Jesus was. You make Jesus a bull rider with a bunch of talented people acting like rodeo clowns ready to come in and grab you up when you fall flat on your ass."

This was the most stimulating conversation I had since Sociology of the Modern Mind. "Who is the bull in your warped sense of my cow dung-type religion?"

"He is the devil you want to scare people who oppose your narrow theology, that is who he is."

My friend could argue violently without ever splitting an infinitive or using a wrong verb tense. Seldom did he slip into vulgarity. His keen mind searched carefully for each word, which came out like a machine gun bullet.

"I guess you think it is wrong to try to use a religious experience for a base to modify human behavior?" I shouted. "What do you think you are doing with your literature courses but turn red-blooded American males into draft-burning freaks who will not fight for their country?"

He looked me square in the eye and said, "Hank, you are not carrying a rifle."

It took me a minute to pull out of that tailspin. "All you want to do is teach D.H. Lawrence's theory that any kind of sexual encounter between human beings is better than an individual taking care of his or her own sex needs."

"Where did you get that idea?"

"From one of your students who told me you interpret Lawrence's story about the little boy who could predict winners of horse races while riding his rocking horse, as a little boy masturbating."

"I merely gave that as one of Lawrence's critic's interpretation. It sounds reasonable."

"Masturbating killing him sounds reasonable? Some medical people are teaching that masturbation is a normal function without harmful effects."

"It isolates the individual from society. People who take care of their own sex drive tend to isolate themselves from other human beings. They become withdrawn loners who stay in isolation from other people. In extreme cases, they become paranoid about their inter actions with other people," the professor went on.

"They do not become pregnant, or catch venereal diseases," I countered.

"That is your opinion."

"No more than it's your opinion an innocent story like The Rocking-Horse Winner is a story about a little boy dying because he played with himself."

"You have read the story?"

"Contrary to what some people think, preachers take about the same courses other people in universities take. It's that we interpret those courses differently."

"I thought God took you out in a desert and filled your minds full of wonderful things that you spend the rest of your life pouring out to your congregation. Some of your people must not have the same knowledge that others do."

"How is that?" I asked.

"Picked up a book in my doctor's office. A preacher wrote it for young boys. He said if boys masturbate, they can never be airplane pilots, or astronauts."

"Guess we would never have anyone flying if that theory holds. I will have to admit, a brain-damaged person is more inclined to carry on excess sexual activity than one who is not. No, we preachers seldom agree about anything. Sometimes, each one of us blames God for our knowledge."

We parted trying to think up our next course of argument. Like two chess players, we studied each move so we could trip up one another. In a town where intellectual talk was at a premium, we sharpened our wits on each other. Sometimes the scars showed.

In all probability, winning the bull riding at the Fort Worth Fat Stock Show did more for my staying for a full five years at Bulton. Their previous pastors had come and gone, usually in one or two years. One had only lasted three months, when he told the deacons he would not preach against some members who were playing golf on Sunday afternoons.

Publicity that I received all over the southwest from that one big event did more for me than any other ride. It was a big Brahma the first ride that did it. Bull name of Hell's Angel caught the crowd's attention. He had never been ridden before. Mean as anything on four hooves, he killed two riders, good ones.

I traded for him. My draw had been a milk cow who calmly ate his hay all the time I studied him. A mild bull can wreck a bull rider in competition. The judges and the crowd do not look with favor on a performance when a bull picks daisies instead of tearing up the arena.

It was a case of wanting to prove to myself that I could ride this bull that caused me to choose him. He lived up to his reputation.

The bull came unwound when they opened the chute. He put his horns between his legs and turned loose. By the time he made two of his moves, I figured him out. Reason no other cowboy had ridden him was that he turned his head the opposite ways from the way he rolled his body in each pitch. All I had to do was follow his opposite direction.

When the whistle blew, I bailed off. There was no use taking any more of that bone-breaking ride than was necessary. Odd thing about it, he did not turn and try to gore me like some did. He shook his horns, knowing he had met his match, and bucked around the arena while he uttered mournful bellers.

There were front page pictures of me in most major papers throughout the southwest. When a college has a winning football season, a coach can do no wrong. Let him lose, they will fire him for blowing his nose the wrong way. That bull was my winning football season at Bulton.

Other rides were child's play after that one. Groups all over asked me to come preach to them. One even paid my way to come to New York for a two-day youth rally.

It was what my ego needed. But it also showed me that my position in the church was on shaky ground if a bull ride could make so much difference in my job. Someday, I was going to be too old for some bull no one else could ride.

It was best to build a solid academic foundation. My major professor already suggested that I stay on and obtain my doctor's degree.

Our group working together was making some real finds in our study of conversion experiences. One man quit bowling after his conversion. We found one in a run-down part of town who had married twice and was sent to prison for molesting a child. This man was now a Baptist preacher.

One thing about Southern Baptist preachers, they are not required to finish any course of formal study. This one had not even finished the third grade. He had taught himself to read while in the pen. Apparently, he was able to hold his job. The church doubled its membership from five hundred to a thousand under his care.

There were five of us in this study group plus the psychiatrist, who were skeptical of this conversion experience. All of us thought more meaningful religious experiences could be brought about with a man of more education in charge.

"Thing I am skeptical of," the psychiatrist observed, "is this man's record of child molesting. A minister has to be in close contact with children. Most of these people think they are cured when they are not. Should he happen to miss sexual fulfillment with his wife or another adult for a period of time, he is apt to revert back to a similar method of fulfilling his sexual appetite."

Since we had to rely on truthfulness of our study group, we had no method of testing the validity of our data. All of our subjects remained anonymous. We made our contacts in such a way that we received our study sheets back in unmarked envelopes.

Our group study had consisted of twenty-five people entirely in Baptist churches. We were starting to broaden our study out to other denominations. It would be an ongoing program that would take years.

"There are some very interesting patterns showing up here," our medical doctor observed. "Should results of conversion ever be predictable, it could be of value in treating behavior problems. Trouble is, as you can see from this limited study, some of these people had very traumatic changes in their lifestyles. Here is one who was a prosperous businessman who gave up his business to work overseas in a mission."

"Is there anything wrong with that?" I asked.

"No. Not unless you were a child in this situation, or a young housewife married to this man and did not care to make this drastic a change."

"Yes, but look at this criminal who was helped to make a drastic change," a graduate student pointed out.

"How permanent is the change in this man?"

"Doctor, he has already done more good in five years after his conversion than he ever did before his change."

"But how much harm can he do if he goes back to his old ways?"

"How secure are any of us in our lives?" I asked.

"What do you mean, Hank?"

"Doctor, take any one of us here, we are each capable of committing a very violent crime, or breaking away from our religious profession and doing harm by our example. Even doctors do some pretty hairy things. Look at what doctors in Germany did during World War II in concentration camps."

"We have had some doctors here who have done things that were awful. One of my acquaintances, who was high in his profession, did a simple operation on a three-year-old girl while drunk. The little girl bled to death," the doctor said.

"So, what is your objection to this criminal holding down a church?" I asked.

"It does not seem right, Hank. There are plenty of you men who are going to be graduating shortly who would like to start working in a church this big. My main concern is whether this man's lifestyle has changed enough to allow him to assume this much responsibility."

We discussed each case with the same amount of thoroughness. After all we said, all of us agreed that on paper, it looked as if we had tested people who had something happen in their minds that was meaningful and helpful to them.

We all knew it was impossible to harness or predict the power that caused this change to come about. Most of us wished society could plug into this power. Only thing, there were good qualities in some of these people which were modified, while there were bad qualities, such as a bad tempers, which were not changed. All I could summarize was we were working with a powerful force that we did not understand.

CHAPTER
NINE

There is much introspective thinking for any minister of the Gospel. A responsible person must realize that he can do much harm through wrong actions.

We had men who, even after they graduated from seminary, found themselves caught up in sexual acts with young boys and girls. Once, a beautiful young girl asked me to have intercourse with her. Never in my time working with people in religious work was I tempted to commit sexual acts with children or young people who were under my charge.

As with most young men, there were strong attractions to the opposite sex. Once, in a revival meeting in a small church, while I was standing in the pulpit, I noticed a buxom woman who greatly resembled Elizabeth Taylor, who always reminded me of a purple grape who needed plucking. Anyway, from my height behind the pulpit, her bosoms showed past her nipples.

It was a short sermon full of hesitations and mistakes. Never did I look in anyone's eyes nor at any woman's tits while preaching after that experience.

After what happened, they tried to prove that my whole ministry had been a time of lecherous activity with various women in the congregation. The charge against me was dropped when the accusers failed to find proof.

It would have disturbed me a great deal if there had been no attraction to those of the opposite sex. In my studies of human sexuality, I noted that some men were attracted sexually to other men. This had never been a problem with me. Never did I say so from the pulpit, but I did not consider this attraction a sin. It was always with great sorrow that I counseled the young men and women who were so inclined.

It had been my policy to try and steer these men and women into more healthy heterosexual relations. My psychiatrist friend told me this was a very dangerous thing to do. "Hank, you are mixing water and oil. All you will do is make two very unhappy people. Unless both parties are homosexual, there will be a problem. Even a bisexual, who is more strongly turned on by his or her friends of the same sex, will seek out sexual partners. In extreme cases, you will have suicides or murder. There was a fine young man attending an eastern seminary who, on his discharge from the military, married a lesbian. She liked to have killed him with a knife on their wedding night."

"What happened to him?" I asked.

"Went back into the Air Force. He was a Lt. Colonel who thought he had a call from God."

"We spent our time here studying about the power of the conversion experience to change people's lives. You will have to admit there has been a noticeable change in some of these peoples' lives. Isn't it possible to change a person from a homosexual to a heterosexual?" I asked.

"That is a hard one to answer. You take a small boy who has had his penis severely mutilated by an over zealous father when he caught his son with a little girl. It is difficult to say whether that man can ever establish a meaningful relationship with a woman. Same way when a little girl is molested by a sadistic man, she may not be able to form a relationship with her husband."

"Do you not think a genuine religious conversion can change the persons involved?"

"Hank, you have to realize there may be physical problems involved that are every bit as severe as Sadie's." We were talking in private. Both of us had formed a trust relationship so we could talk freely. "There have even been studies that seem to indicate a homosexual's body hormones are different."

"I know your story about punishment does not always hold

water. A friend of mine started having sexual relations with a neighbor's girl when both of them were very small. Their parents beat the hell out of those children. When they grew up, they married each other. They now have several children of their own," I said.

"There are exceptions to the rule, Hank. Every person reacts to circumstances differently."

"How do you handle homosexuals in your practice?"

"Very distantly. No, I have found it best to help them adjust to their lifestyle without feeling a great deal of guilt."

"This state has laws against it," I pointed out.

"This state has laws against a lot of things it does not enforce."

"Guess I will continue to pray with people who come to me for help," I decided, since there did not seem to be any better treatment.

"Unless your inclinations are that way, be very careful. Some are very brilliant and charming people with a lot of achievements."

"I cannot see myself falling in love with a man."

"Hank, I cannot either, from what we discussed about you."

When Eastern New Mexico came down to play Texas Central, my loyalties lay with my alma mater. No matter how hard Kent and I tried, we were unable to bring ourselves to sit and cheer against the green and silver.

Our choice of football teams did not cause near the amount of trouble it did when I refused to preach a sermon on the doctrine of creationism as opposed to evolution.

Bill North came while I was seated in my study. He knocked on the fake oak and I invited him in. "Hank, you got by with about anything you wanted to do."

This was a familiar message. "Bill, what do they want me to do now?"

"Preach against evolution."

"I was not there when it happened, Bill."

"You read your Bible."

"The Bible does not say anything about how God created the world, just by whom."

"What do you mean? It flatly states in Genesis, God created it in six days and rested on the seventh."

"Where does it say there were twenty-four hour days?" I asked.

"Are you trying to argue for evolution?"

"Not arguing for anything. Evidence gathered by scientists seems to favor a creation over several million years."

"If the board of deacons hears of you being an atheistic evolutionist, they will fire you."

"Did you hear me say I was an evolutionist?" I asked.

"Then, why will you not preach against it?"

"I do not know which is right. No one does."

"A good Christian knows right from wrong."

"Some good Christians get themselves in a lot of trouble meddling in things that they should leave alone. There are some devout Christians who believe in evolution," I told him.

"My Bible is clear as water that God created the world in 4004 B.C. You cannot deny that, Hank."

"Some things should have never been put in the Bible. Bishop Ussher put that in many years later. How he got his figures no one is sure, but he seems to have taken figures given in the Bible about when each family named in David's and Christ's ancestry lived and come up with this date."

"You are trying to tell me everything in my Bible is not true?" He was beginning to get riled up about my answers.

"I'm trying to tell you some things were put in our Bible by men who had a bone to pick. Trouble with you, Bill, is that you want cut and dried answers for every problem. If you cannot answer it from the Bible, you sink. God gave us brains to use; use yours."

"Take it by this, Hank, you are not going to preach against evolution."

"I will preach that I believe God had a hand in creating the universe, but when and how He did it has nothing to do with my belief."

"I will tell the deacons what you said. They may ask you to resign."

"Bill, read this letter."

"It looks personal. One of those big Dallas churches offering you twice what you are getting here? You are trying to blackmail us."

"No. You are trying to threaten me. I am defending myself by saying there are other churches than First Baptist, Bulton."

It worked. I heard later that Bill talked them out of firing me. They used it as testimony against me later. The State did not care whether I believed in evolution or not. There were other charges brought against me by the church that did matter.

You will think my days at Bulton were full of church quarrels. That was not true at all. There were times when we had long periods of peace, when church affairs went like clockwork. My memories of those wonderful people are still fresh in my mind. They did many nice things for me, and we had times of comradeship when it seemed that God came down and sat in on our services.

Some of you who read this will not believe in God either. There were times when I did not, but now I do even more than when it all happened.

Sadie and I were having our quiet time together one late spring day before the seminary granted my undergraduate degree in the May commencement.

The world had come back to life again, with honeybees and yellowjackets droning 'round the birdbath. Winter birds left for colder climates. Our bluejays and mocking birds were flitting around in the trees. A mockingbird was on top of our television antenna singing his songs.

Under the crepe myrtle bush, a black and white cat tried to pounce on a sparrow, who flitted from bird seed to seed, trying to peck a few here and there. Sadie pulled out a light pair of binoculars, which she could handle, to watch this feline creature.

"Want me to chase him away?"

"No, Hank, it seems to me cats have a place in the scheme of things. Perhaps there would be too many sparrows if they were not there."

"Guess your parents and my mother will be here next week for graduation," I said.

"Give anything to go. Life seems to get tiresome sometimes, but there are so many things to do here that I shan't complain."

She never did. "See your book is getting highest acclaim."

"Enjoyed doing that more than anything I have ever done. Transcendentalism. Thought myself back into Christ's time and wrote it from His viewpoint."

"Careful, Emerson. You will lose yourself sometime," I joked.

"Hank, it is good having you here making fun of me again. Like old times. It would be nice to be back in New Mexico. My favorite time was spring."

"Same here. Remember how helpless those little calves looked? Mother wrote they had a ninety-nine percent calf crop this year with a good spring rain. Ever wish we had not left?"

She answered, "Selfishly, yes. It would have been good to have stayed home with you as my husband. For Bulton and some parts of the southwest where you have worked, no. It would have been such a waste of time."

"Professor laid out my course of study for my doctorate."

"Tell me about it, Hank. It excites me so. Move over here closer. What area are you going to be working in?"

"Psychology of Religion. They are going to let me expand my project on conversion. We are thinking about going into a depth study with a doctor supervising our interviews. We are considering using drugs and hypnosis. There is some data being collected in mental hospitals."

"What do you mean, Hank?"

"Ex-soldiers in V.A. hospitals are being monitored on their religious experiences. There are some negative effects from conversion. We need to know what they are so reliable ministers can watch for them."

"How about where they are trying to brainwash some of these cult members who they are trying to bring back into mainstream society?"

I answered, "Only reason it is so difficult to find out anything from most mental health facilities is there is such a feeling of disgust between members of the two opposing forces."

"Disgust?" she asked.

"Yes. At one time mental hospitals used religious workers to bring people back to reality. Ministers took advantage of this in order to try and gain converts. Without considering the individual's needs, they treated everyone the same. They tried to offer one placebo conversion. Many mental illness symptoms are results of disease or injuries. A hell fire sermon did not heal all of them. It only made them worse. Once trained mental health workers got rid of religious workers, they threw the good out with the bad."

"Sounds reasonable, Hank. What does that have to do with your program?"

"They do not want us messing with their patients, especially with patients who have already had traumatic religious experiences."

"Seems like they have thrown the baby out with the bath water, doesn't it?" she asked.

"It always happens in a reform. No one wants religious trained workers anymore. Most state universities will almost forbid a religious discussion in their classrooms so superiors cannot accuse them of a conflict between church and state."

"At Eastern they allowed discussions of Communism and every other `ism' along with religion. It is a stupid reaction, Hank."

We continued our conversation throughout the meal. In some ways, our sharing of ideas took the place of the sexual sharing we could not engage in. I looked forward to our times together, but I did not extend them or encourage more frequent visits. Sadie's health was failing. There were dark circles under her eyes. It hurt me to see this beautiful woman wasting away before my eyes.

Her mother came more often. It seemed that she could do things with Sadie that the rest of us could not. She could encourage her to eat enough to live on. At times, it seemed that before our very eyes, she was losing her will to fight and live. It was only her fight to write that kept her alive.

There was graduation and then a six-day fishing trip, after which there was the Southern Baptist Convention in San Francisco. This was a trip I was looking forward to. I had heard that there were plans afoot to elect me president of this august body.

Church politics are boring to those not on the inside. There were more intrigues and clever manipulations in church elections than in national elections. There were stories of ballot box stuffing, and of those who would bring street people in to cast their votes. If half of the tales are true, it is frightening.

The Southern Baptists started the Convention before the Civil War, when agitation had increased between North and South. Only Southern states were involved. As the western expansion pushed to the Pacific, far-sighted church leaders saw that it was necessary to expand along with those members who were casting their lives into a new society. Southern Baptists moved west.

During the two World Wars, Southern people went north to work in steel mills, rubber plants, sewing factories, and assembly plants, especially automobile manufacturing plants around Detroit. They were Rosie the Riveters in shipyards. Hollywood drew its share when this vast empire called on southerners to build its props, write its scripts and clean up its messes. Some of them were the actors and actresses in this grist mill.

Southern Baptist ministers migrated north and west to keep watch over their flock.

All of this is necessary to understand why my name was up for nomination that year. My name was a byword like Billy Sunday's had been a generation before. A bull rider, they invited me to every major church gathering in the south and west. Little boys had posters of me in their bedrooms. There was one of me sitting a bull while reading my Bible. Mothers loved me for the positive influence on their ornery boys.

On the other hand, there were those in the convention who were trying to fight the extreme Fundamentalist movement, which was sweeping the Denomination and tearing it limb from limb. My stand on evolution, separation of church and state, and my work on the scientific study of the conversion experience had swept the intellectual community behind the education of this vast denomination.

A conservative evangelist, this was what was needed to bring the fighting factions together. There was also a need for a well-known figure, clean from scandal, who could help reunite a giant torn apart when electronic ministers started hauling in millions to carry on their enterprises of hospitals and schools.

Like a leech on a blind man, this tremendous siphoning of money into non-related denominational work was drying up Southern Baptist universities, hospitals, churches and missions. I was their ace in the hole. Perhaps I could have become the Billy Graham of the South, if things had only gone right.

CHAPTER
TEN

After marching across the stage and shaking hands with Billy Graham at our commencement ceremony, there were honors for academics and for achievements in religious fields. They named me most outstanding undergraduate of Southwestern Baptist Theological Seminary that year. My three parents sat in front row seats, while officials bestowed honors on me. I earned the privilege of wearing the red shawl across my shoulders, which signified my position in the educational system.

It was the end of three grueling years of intensive study that added to my Bachelor of Arts, a Master of Theology. Two more years of intensive study would earn me a Doctor of Theology. Some of these initials after ministers' names, like D.D., are merely window drapings given by grateful colleges or universities. Some ministers wear letters granted by diploma mills, which give high-sounding titles for as little as five hundred dollars. It is the shame and disgrace of the charlatans who walk among us. But, then who am I to condemn other men?

It was a busy day. Three morning services, a quick trip to Fort Worth for graduation, a hurried up evening service, then it was off to Padre Island until the next Saturday, when I would come back to rest for the following Sunday. This was the way I took my vacations for five years at Bulton. One thing they did not accuse me of at the trial was being lazy.

There was a last minute meeting with Kent, then a hurried good-bye with Sadie and our parents. She was to have their company until I came back. I tried to persuade her father to come with me in my new motor home, which had been my graduation present.

"No Hank," he said, "you go ahead and enjoy yourself. I will stay here and visit with Sadie. Maybe we can run over to Lake Proctor and fish or something an afternoon before I leave. I am proud of you, Son. Almost as proud as I would be if you and Sadie were living on the ranch."

It was an all night drive, but in spite of my fatigue, I was too wound up to want a quick nap along the highway in a rest stop.

First rays of morning found me at the Bob Hall pier, which stretches out into the Gulf. Already there were early morning fishermen lined up along this vast wooden structure, which points a finger far out into the Gulf of Mexico.

There were people emerging from little sleeping shelters along the beach. Females in skimpy bathing suits skimmed over the beach looking for sea shells washed in by the night's rising tide.

It is seldom in the late spring a visitor to Texas beaches finds ideal conditions for surf fishing. Usually, inland storms or storms out in the Gulf mess up the indigo blue of this vast ocean water and shore feeding fish pull out to deeper water until the silt subsides.

Conditions were perfect. A gentle swell broke the coastline; early morning bathers waded out past the fishing pier to let giant waves carry them in towards shore.

Not wanting vacationing sun bathers to disturb me, I headed the motor home, which was equipped with four-wheel-drive, down towards Mexico. It was a good ten miles I went on down south towards where, in early days, a priest ran a cattle ranch.

The Texas coast is like a woman, beautiful, yet deceptive. This narrow strip of sand that I traveled stretches like a barrier from south of Corpus to Mexico. It looks like a perfect highway of white beach sand bounded by giant sand dunes on the west and blue Gulf water on the east.

Stay on wet sand, you are safe. Get off the well-packed sand, your vehicle bogs. Even in a four-wheel-drive recreational vehicle, you will sink down into loose sand until the vehicle's frame rests on shifting sand.

Get too close to water, and your vehicle will bog down into salty

Gulf water and be eaten away by the rolling tide. It is only safe to travel this fisherman's paradise during calm weather. A violent thunderstorm and the beach becomes a raging maelstrom of water beating all across and over the sand dunes. People have been marooned for days. Some have paid with their lives.

I pulled onto a neck of hard-packed sand without another vehicle in sight. This area was away from beach- combers out for morning strolls. Far to the north, there was one isolated camper who, like me, sought privacy from society.

Along the sand dunes, even this early in the growing season, sea oats were lending their greenness to giant morning glories, which sent their tenacious runners into the loose sand, holding the dunes in place for another season of restless footsteps and churning sand buggies wanting to tear up this natural barrier.

Up and down the beach there were the dregs of a society that did not mind contaminating its natural resources with empty beer bottles, wrecked tankers, and all the other millions of containers and junk that can sweep up onto a nation's natural park.

Old shoes curled under a relentless sun, while here and there lay giant logs washed from some inland woodland. Near me there lay a cottonwood tree trunk with sand washed up against it. Last summer it had been up the Nueces River, far inland. It had leaned over a shallow creek, where it had stood for two centuries. That spring torrents of water had washed it roaring down into the flood-swollen river and carried it out to the raging Gulf, where finally it had been swept ashore and left abandoned on Padre Island's barren seashore.

There were blackened areas on its silvery-gray wood, where parties of young people had tried to burn its hard surface so that they could roast their wieners and toast their buns, while they sat sipping out of beer bottles. In a few years, the giant tree would be buried deep under layer after layer of sand, which would gather around and over its hoary root system that was now exposed to the elements.

One violent winter's storm and nature's forces would take care of the filth and debris man had left on its unmarked expanse of drifting sand. Once again, like a school boy's new Chief tablet, there would be no marks of contamination on this marred beach.

There was a taste of sea water in my mouth. The cleansing salt water washed away all of winter's accumulation of hurts from my sinus cavities and aching bones.

Fighting sleep, I stripped, drew on a pair of trunks, put my feet into new canvas deck shoes and hit the gentle surf with all caution thrown to the breeze. I carelessly waded out into water that barely reached my knees, until I got out into the pounding surf far offshore.

Breaking all rules of good safety, I fell into long, rolling waves and was swept closer into shore. Large fish and seaweed brushed against my bare skin. Swimming with my face drenched in salt water, I forgot all cares until, glancing up, off in the blue water, an ominous black fin cut through the frothing surf.

Then I remembered the warnings against swimming so far out away from crowds, who would scare these monsters of the deep. Careful not to attract attention, I beat a retreat shoreward. Long before I could reach harbor, there was a mighty rush of a beating fish body. This monster snatched a morsel of finny meat out of the brine not ten feet from me.

It was like sitting, once again, on the rolling bull, but this time there was no cheering crowd to encourage my endeavors. Slowly and deliberately I faced this meat-tearing creature from the deep without even a knife in my trembling hands.

It flashed through my mind, "Would I die out here alone in this foaming surf? Would this be the end, a quick attack by this man-eating shark and then a froth of bloody water to be swept inward to stain the grayish-white beach? Who would take care of Sadie?" my mind was pounding as I fought panic.

Once again there was a mighty rush towards me. It was as if a guardian angel turned aside this messenger of death to cause it to find another fish in the surf. I at last found myself in water barely knee-deep. Again, the monster struck behind me. A wallowing wave brought enough water to float huge, gnashing beast in towards shore.

While he feasted, I backed hurriedly towards shore. The frothing blood from my adversary's kills were attracting other black fins, which cut the water closer and closer to me. It was then that a wave swept me off my feet and I went towards shore at a violent pace, while one ferocious fish made a slash at my buttocks. There was an angry gash along my thigh when the wave receded and shallow water forced the fish to go back into the swelling surf.

After dressing my stinging wound, I watched while a milling malady of black fins cut in and through the surf catching threshing fish while over and over again they struck at fish splashing in the blood-curled surf.

Sea gulls and lesser sea birds darted and swooped into the frothing tide to pick up morsels of fish that the flesh-tearing sharks ignored as they chased bigger prey. Occasionally, a gaping mouthful of gnashing teeth would break the surface. A shark would take a hundred pound fish and lift it above the water, fighting to eat it while it struggled.

It was as if I were mesmerized into inactivity while I watched this ferocious attack. What a sight. Peaceful, frantic fish tried to swim up on dry sand to escape their gnashing foes.

After the feeding frenzy ended, I went back to my camper, and, pulling off my bloody trunks, I fell exhausted onto my bunk and slept.

A hot, south Texas sun bore down on me when I finally got up and prepared a light bait-casting rig for action. My first choice was a silver spoon designed to catch speckled trout.

Fear gripping my mind, I waded into the receding surf with caution. Making sure there were no sharks in view, I carefully cast my bait into the glass-blue water, broken only by the fine marbling of white foam.

There was a calmness to the water that belied what had happened that morning. It was on my third cast, a swirling in the water was followed by my pole bending double. The line sang when I let it, until, with a flip of my thumb, the star brake caused the charging fish to stop his pell-mell journey towards open water.

My fish came in fighting until, with a sudden ease, it lost all fight and I drew it on in. It was my habit to bring only a few cans of food and catch the rest of my meals from the Gulf water.

It is strange about sea life. Much of it is so fragile. Leave it in its natural habitat and it can live for years, but pull it towards land, and some things die before they reach shore. It seems they would rather die than let man take them out of their salty world.

My next cast brought in a struggling sheet of commercial plastic, washed in from some industrial site. Most things, even iron, will eventually disintegrate in Gulf waters. Plastic will not. It is the fisherman's curse. Catch it on your hook, it will make your pole act as if it hooked into a likely fish. At last, when you bring it in, it turns out to be nothing but a useless piece of trash.

From my observations and reading, it seems that the ocean is fairly self cleaning. Think of all the human waste, industrial material, and chemical run-offs that dump daily in rivers far from the ocean. Most of it eventually runs into salt water. Here, its decomposition starts when nature tries to keep the saline water from becoming a giant cesspool, where nothing will grow but undesirable weeds and some rough fish with cast-iron intestines.

As oxygen furnishing plants die out, the fish that depend on those plants die out. How long will it be, at our present rate of dumping phosphates, petrocarbons and other toxic material into the ocean, before we no longer have a viable ocean? Perhaps we will kill it off this next winter, or perhaps it will still be sloshing against the seashore long after man has killed himself off in some freak war or nuclear accident.

No matter how durable the ocean is, it is very trying for the fisherman to pull in piece after piece of industrial plastic that takes years to disintegrate. Will we eventually have an ocean full of plastic that will foul up all ships' screws until they can no longer move? Perhaps my experience with the shark caused my bad frame of mind.

By the time I caught four trout, the evening sun was a red ball of fire in the western sky, then the rolling tide started coming in towards shore again.

After I built a roaring fire out of driftwood, I prepared my fish and canned beans. Darkness settled down across the land, closing off all visibility except flickering campfires here and there in the darkness.

Far off in the distance, offshore drilling rigs still sent their beacons of light into a dark horizon. Far to the north, the fishing pier lights twinkled a necklace of lights in the water.

Closer to me, about a mile away, a bonfire similar to mine cast leaping flames into a dark night sky. Sparks shot off into the blackness as if the air was alive with brightness.

There was always a period after dark on the beach when a melancholy came over me, causing me to fall into deep thought. It was at this time that I always thought most about Sadie. Her warmth, denied me these years, brought my thoughts back to the mountains that summer. I wondered how our lives would have been had this dreadful thing not happened to us.

Each night at this time, my anxiety for Sadie increased until it tempted me to get in my vehicle and head north towards home.

She scolded me severely the first night I did this, when I camped on a lake closer to home. When I walked in the door, she said, "Hank, you are going to drive both of us crazy with your worrying. I enjoy life. You are not going to make yourself miserable following after me." She sent me back camping that night.

She had an inner calmness that helped me find myself. It was while I was out there in murky darkness that we communed with each other across the vast distance that separated us.

Sometimes a morbid feeling of the accident being all my fault came over me. To break off those periods of self accusation, I turned my idle mind to better employment.

Going into my mobile home, I found a book that I would use next Sunday for services. Although inspiration often came to me for sermons, it was still with a great deal of checking facts and writing rough drafts that I carefully prepared every sermon. Never in all the times I spoke, did a sermon get preached without my spending hours of preparation. Although I never spoke from a written draft, I never went into the pulpit without a fully drafted, typed sermon, even when the program was only an informal speech out under a western sky.

My sermons are in cardboard filing boxes. Perhaps someday I will publish them so future generations can study my style. Some will say that is vain, but my sermons have stirred thousands when God poured his thoughts through my voice.

When sleep finally closed my mind, there was still a blazing campfire in the immediate distance. Before going to sleep, I walked up and down along the wet sand. The changing of the ocean tide brought water nearer and nearer to my campsite.

Instead of sleeping in the close confines of a restricted vehicle, I unrolled a sleeping bag onto a plastic sheet. I drifted off into a deep sleep.

Sadie came to me in my dreams and told me how much she cared for me. She was still in her unbroken body, which I had loved since first I remember. She drew her body close to mine, and there was relief for my throbbing thoughts that night.

CHAPTER
ELEVEN

It is time to tell what happened. Even after a year (or is it two?) it seems so unreal, as if the whole thing had happened in a dream.

The next morning, before there was much more than a pink thinge far out to sea, my eyes came open with the realization that a figure stood over me in the half dawn.

"I am so lonesome," a pleasant sounding woman's voice came to me out of the gloom. "I've been camped up here for two weeks without seeing or talking to another human being."

Surprise wore off to wonderment. While my racing mind filled in gaps. "Let me put some clothes on and I will build us a fire."

"No, that is all right. Stay in your bedroll; I will sit here and talk, if you do not mind. My name is Mary. There is more, but for now this is enough for you to know."

"Live around here, Mary? I am Hank."

"Sounds like a dog's name," she said with a gentle laugh. "No, I live on a lake up close to Fort Worth."

"I am from Bulton. Pastor of First Baptist Church."

"About twenty miles from my home. I am sure you are married."

"Yes. Sadie is an invalid. You may have heard about her, a bull hit her in the arena over at Fort Worth."

"Of course. You are that Hank."

"Seems you know quite a bit about me already, which is more than I can say about you. I am being awfully impolite. Sit down here on the edge of my sleeping bag so you won't get sand on you."

There was enough light now that it was possible to see that she was a few years older than me. Her hair looked dark with a reddish tinge. She was a short, well-built woman with a beach robe over her garments. Somehow, I knew she was a decent person.

When she carefully sat down, her robe came apart, exposing well formed thighs clad in a very brief bathing suit. I remembered my psychiatrist friends warning about me coming apart if I ever let myself go. All kinds of warnings came into my system; signals went off telling me to be careful.

"Tell me about yourself, Mary. It is not often I am awakened by a beautiful woman standing over me."

"Your wife a complete invalid?"

"Bedfast since the accident. You have a husband?"

"Not anymore."

"Divorced?"

"No, he died in Vietnam. Flew a bomber. Last mission he did not come back."

"MIA?"

"No, they recovered his body and sent it home. He made full Colonel. The Air Force was to send him home and give him a desk job after his mission. He never made it. I like to come here and remember him like he was when we married, a young pilot fresh out of West Point. He transferred to the Air Cadets. We stayed married eight years. This is our anniversary."

"Children?"

"No. My fault. Something is backward in me."

"You do not look backward."

"Thank you. You are from New Mexico. Eastern New Mexico. Quarterback for the Greyhounds. All-'round cowboy for two years."

"You know a lot about me."

"John did some work in Albuquerque. He read the sports page like a Bible. Strange that I should use that expression to a minister."

"Quite all right."

It would have been only natural that she undress and crawl into my sleeping bag with me. She might have thought about it, but it did not happen that way. She turned her head until I slipped on my trunks over my nudeness. We both giggled about out lack of modesty.

There was a slight coolness in the air, which the sun's hot rays would soon change. There is nothing more beautiful than a sunrise along the beach. Sun starts coming up like a big red balloon with a hazy mist covering its face. It seems to stand there suspended in space, as if it will never come on over the horizon.

Coleridge's description always came to mind, "Like a painted ship on a painted ocean." All eternity stopped while we looked at each other in this early light of the unreal world, where shadows appeared to be substance and substance appeared to be shadows.

Out over the water, water fowl started their squalls. Sea gulls circled us as though they suspected our relationship of being more than it was. Up on the sand dune a cow nursed her calf. There was a quiteness about the pastoral scene that bespoke something that was to be.

"Race you to the surf," she said. She cast her robe down on my sleeping bag. There was a startling beauty about her that caused me to feel her deep down in my thighs. She did not mind my looking at her. In fact, she seemed to want my assessment of her full breast and figure. She was one of the most beautiful women I had ever seen.

We made it to the water when she glanced at my lacerated thigh. Kneeling down on wet sand, she carefully ran her fingers over the fresh wound. It was as though electric current ran from her body into mine. My hands went onto her bent head, and she wrapped her arms around my hips.

She looked into my face. Her lips were sensuous when I pulled her up to me and brought my mouth down on hers, first gently, and then, when we connectd, very hard. She pressed her body against mine, while our hands played with each other. She found my manliness with her cupped hand and gently massaged. We stayed together for long enough to let the sun come up half-way out of silvery water. It was as though we had known each other for a lifetime.

"Did it hurt when you skinned yourself?"

"Shark hit me yesterday."

"Really? It looked like a battle ground out there. I have heard of them coming in close here, but never have I seen them before," she said.

She once again knelt to examine the strange scars. Her head pressed against me. As I started to sink towards her, she leaped up and ran towards the water. Her feet made sucking sounds when she ran into the silent surf, where little lines moved back and forth, as water lapped at the shore and then receded. There was a white foam marking last night's high tide.

I caught her. We splashed through the surf for a short distance. She placed her hand in mine. It was going to be a different relationship than Sadie and I had. She was asking for it.

We raced outward into deep water. Our bodies found each other in a swelling wave, and we clung together. My hand went down into her halter top. Her breast was firm in my massaging hand. As the water receded, my lips found their way to the cleavage between her breasts and then moved over so I could listen to her rapidly beating heart.

She did not protest when I took her halter top off and looked at her full nakedness there in the light of morning. A new life came into me. The thrill of seeing a new breast brought me ready. Surely she would not pull away from me, or say, "No, Hank," like every other woman had done.

Instead, she reached her hand down into my trunks. We stood together. Waves rose round us and then receded and came round us again.

"Hank, let's walk up the beach a ways. I want to get acquainted with you better, before...." She did not finish her sentence, but I knew we were going to be lovers before long.

"Tie my halter back in case someone drives by."

"No one did yesterday."

"No one usually comes down this far during the week. There were some sand vehicles went by late Sunday. They have not been back."

Reluctantly, I tied her halter back, but before I completed the job, my hands were on her again, and this time they did not stop with her breasts.

She braced against me, and we explored each other. There was a fulfillment in me that I had never known before. "Come on, Hank, I want to walk a little more first."

We walked short distance and then stopped, while we found each other again and again. Neither of us minded our wet bodies; we pressed ourselves closer and closer together.

There is a thrill that can never be recaptured at the first time a man and woman disrobe before each other. She examined me. "You are still a virgin, Hank," she said in amazement. "We are going to get caught out here like this. You are not going to let me walk. We better go back before a beach patrol picks us up for indecent exposure."

She was not vulgar with her loving. All that I knew was that I wanted her every bit as bad as she wanted me. Somehow it was as if we bouth knew we were meant for each other.

Neither of us could keep our hands off the other. We like to have never made it to my place. Casting our clothes aside, we stood in sunlight looking at one another.

"You are beautiful," I said.

"Oh, Hank, I never expected anything like this."

"Hurry inside. It would not be right for me to take you out here in the open."

"Why?" she teased me.

We pulled the sleeping bag round out of view, and when she pulled me down on her I knew my first woman. It lasted a long time. After we finished, we lay in each other's arms, not caring to break the spell.

Why do people think sex is dirty? This was an experience of shere ecstasy. She lay trying to arouse me again. Finally, she brought her body on top of me, and once again she started working againt me.

It was past noon before we finished. Both of us were spent.

"Hank, you look famished. We better get some food in you quick. What do you have?"

"You ought to know."

"I'm talking about food, smart aleck," she said.

"There are eggs. Trout should still be fresh, iced."

When she rose to leave, my hand found her body, and she came against me again for a brief moment before she gently pushed me away and went to cook us food over smoldering embers.

We like to have never cooked our first meal. First it was her and then it was me. We kept coming to each other for more and more.

Things we did to and for each other would make up a book. Most of that day we stayed undressed, or in various stages of undressing. Some of it is a blur, but we walked over the sand dunes to a clump of salt cedar that grew out of the marshland. We made it through the brackish waste to the trees, when a slight rustling brought us to our senses.

There were seven or eight mother cow circled 'round, watching us in wonderment. I still had not finished for the fifth time, but we had to lie and laugh at this strange audience, whose eyes showed faint flickers of forgotten affairs they had had with willing bulls last fall.

"I am spoiling your fishing trip, Hank."

"You are making my trip." I pulled her down against me gently, and she sought to please me. It was as if both of us had known each other for a lifetime, yet it was as though we had just met and were trying our best to know each other better.

We talked between times. She told me about John a little. "Hank, I almost killed myself when it happened. It was not like some of those wives who still do not know whether their husbands are alive or not. It was a sense of unreality. He came to me in the dark asking for help. Once I was on the plane with him. He pushed me out before we crashed. He said good-bye before I parachuted to safety. After that, he did not come again.

"There was plenty of money. His parents left him wealthy. I wanted to get as far away as possible from roaring airplanes and military. That was when I bought my place on a hillside overlooking a lake. My home is up on top of a steep hill with cedar growing all around. You can stop by on our way home."

It saddened me that there would be a time when we would have to go home. It was Tuesday. Three days, short now, stretched out before us.

Our first night together was a thing of ecstasy. We lay on my sleeping bag out under open skies. After our first lovemaking, stars were shining brilliantly above our heads. We lay looking up at them while we quietly pulled and tugged at each other's bodies.

For the first time in my life, I was able to express how I felt about life, the part a man tells only to a woman, the right woman.

We finished for the second time and went for a midnight swim. This time we did not bother with swimming suits. We waded through the surf, knowing that any minute we might step on a stingray or brush against a jellyfish. We threw all caution away as we found each other in the pounding surf. The gentle lapping of the water added to our complete enjoyment.

We stayed in the water a long time. There was no sleep in us. Once, the magic moment broke when I thought of Sadie, who would never be able to satisfy me the way this woman did. Still there was sudden feeling of guilt, when my body shuddered in its last fulfillment of the moment.

"Something wrong, Hank? You are thinking of Sadie, aren't you? Talk about her; sometimes it helps."

I found myself for the first time pouring out all that had happened and how, every time I looked at her, it hurt me until there was a numbness that caused a pain down into my heart.

"Let us go to bed, Hank. It is getting cold."

We found sleep at last, with both of us curled against each other. She was still asleep when I carefully disentangled myself and built a fire. When she awoke there was a frying pan full of brown fish and fried eggs.

We did not dress that day. It was as if we were primitive savages enjoying an Eden where people had never invented clothing.

There are indentations between the dunes that form totally isolated sand valleys. We explored one of these. Digging down in the sand, we dug out sea shells buried by a raging tide, which, during a hurricane, had pushed sea life over this coastal basin.

There were things to see and explore besides ourselves. Both of us were modest people ordinarily. It was as if we had each found a person with whom we could be entirely ourselves. We pushed away all inhibitions.

"Read to me out of your Bible, Hank."

"Why?"

"I want you to. Here, wrap this towel around you. It would be best that you are not seen that way."

We spent the rest of that morning reading each other parts of the Bible we liked best. I read her Song of Solomon. We both became aroused by the sensual imagery of the young lover flattering his beloved with his golden tongue.

"You think that is a Christian piece of literature?" she asked me.

"You mean, should it be in the Biblical canon because it is a love song of Christ to his church?"

"Something like that, Hank."

We had finished our lovemaking that was started by this beautiful love poem. I was rubbing tanning lotion on her body.

"It is purely a sensuous piece of literature that every person should read, my beloved. Christians cannot stand to have sexual beauty in their reading. Some have such guilt feelings when they confront their own sexuality that they have to turn everthing into a religious allegory."

Mary read me the story of Ruth in its entirely. A sense of the beauty of this simple piece of literature came over me that I had never felt before. Her voice was like the mockingbird trilling out into the morning air.

We grew drowsy and napped a spell. Awaking with the noon sun beaming brightly down on our bare bodies, I said, "Mary, we'd better go and get out of this heat before we get sunstroke. Good thing both of us tanned before this. The worst burn a person can get is out on this sand."

We lay under the shade of a piece of canvas stretched from the camper body to two poles driven in the sand.

We were still in total isolation. It was as if we were the only man and woman alive in a vast expanse of water and sea. Under the noon sun we lay napping.

A blowfly circled, singing its droning song of monotony as it dipped and whirled in the hot sun. Faint breezes drifted sand across our blanket. The dunes were now a simmering expanse of sand

115

stretching across our horizon.

Far overhead a jet cut its contrails across an unmarked blue sky. We could look out over the eastern horizon towards the never-silent Gulf, which stretched into the sky, where both came together in a meeting not broken by any human thing, until a fishing boat occasionally appeared on the horizon, breaking a vast expanse of void into a realistic scene with human-made things marring its surface.

Once, during the short afternoon, a ship appeared on the horizon. It churned its relentless journey towards some goal that only it knew about. A small Navy vessel went by shortly afterwards. It looked like a destroyer.

"I can see why a person could go stark raving mad here, Hank."

"Are you going mad, Mary?"

"No, but imagine being marooned here without human companion for a month or a year. Storms cast some of the early explorers up on this beach without any food or clothing. Cabeza de Vaca went across this wilderness with only a servant. He walked all way up into Kansas and then over a continent to the Pacific."

"Bet his feet got sore," I said.

"As a matter of fact, they did. The only thing that kept him going were friendly Indians who used him to heal them."

"Oral Roberts of his day."

"Really, Hank, his journal records incidents of laying his hands on sick people and healing them."

I said, "So does Joseph Smith, when he first started the Mormon Church. Early missionaries into new countries have reported this amazing ability that Paul seemed to have passed on."

"You heal me, Hank, when you lay your hands on my body. I was afraid you would be a rapist or a murderer when I came down here. It was an awful risky thing to do."

"I agree with you, but I enjoy your company. You did not get raped, either."

"I have been awfully well used."

"Not any more than I have been." I went over and pulled her close to me. We spent the heat of the day talking and making love.

116

She got up and fixed us cool lemonade and opened a can of pork and beans, only she did something to it that made it more than pork and beans. We laughed while we fed each other from our one spoon.

Late that afternoon, we baited our surf-casting equipment and, covering ourselves with our dry swimming clothes, we caught fish for the evening meal.

Most of what we caught, we tossed back. Both of us caught hard heads that croaked when we used leather gloves to take them off the hooks. The slimy catfish looked with pitiful eyes while we worked to get our hooks back.

Evening was drawing its velvet shades over sand and water when finally we caught two, medium-sized sand sharks, who fought our tugging lines all the way to shore.

Both of them together weighed over twenty pounds. Small ones. This species seldom attacks humans.

It was short work. I used a pair of pliers to pull their tough hides down over their tail fins.

Hooking up a spit over a smoldering fire built in a trench, we allowed our meal to cook to a slow brown. We dug our green roasting ears and whole potatoes out of hot sand and prepared our evening meal.

"This shark meat's good, Hank."

"People been throwing it away for years. Go around where there is a bunch fishing, you will find their catch rotting on the beach. First time I was down here, I cooked one of these small ones. It was the most delicious thing I ever tasted."

"It is good. No bones hardly at all." she said between mouthfuls.

"No, just a series of small bones down their vertebrae. Everything else is tough cartilage."

"Thing I always heated about fish," she said, "those little bones are so aggravating. This has a toughness to it like steak."

"Only thing about it, it will spoil fast. You will not know you've eaten contaminated shark unitl an hour or so later, when you start losing your toenails through your mouth. I do not know if people die from it, but I felt like it would have been a relief." The thought of what happened still made me sick.

"Found out lots of things people throw out are really good food if fixed right. There is enough food wasted on this earth to feed everyone if it could be distributed equally. There is no sense in anyone going to bed hungry, or of little children having swollen stomachs and pipestems for legs. What happens? We put it in concrete storage tanks to rot. Think of all the grain turned back into alcohol, so people can become ill and drunk." I said.

"Wonder if foreign nations will ever let us come in and feed their people adequatley. It seems they think it is an entrapment, Hank. We feed them today and make slaves out of them tomorrow."

"Seems like we did it, Mary. In the past we fed people, got them dependent on us and then exploited their natural resources for our own gain. We did not colonize for the good of undeveloped countries."

"I remember in college reading about us trying to ship free grain into India to feed their hungry people. Hank, their farmers revolted because they said their price of rice went kaput."

"Guess there is no way to do anything but follow the crowd and let people starve," I said sadly.

They testifed at the trail that we had clandestine meetings where we met to have sex orgies. Some said they saw us running around naked out in the open.

There is no guilt from what Mary and I did. She loved me and I loved her. My only regret with our affair was that it was not Sadie who was with me those short nights when we satisfied each other.

CHAPTER
TWELVE

Beachcombing, we walked through deep sand exploring tree trunks and metal tanks cast upon the beach. She was walking, following in my footsteps. She stretched her legs for the long steps. Turning around, I saw a tear in her eye. "Must you go home today, Hank?" It was early Saturday morning, shortly after dawn.

She had put on one of my old shirts over her bikini. There was a chill in the early morning air. I was as sad as she, only it did not show as much.

"Darling, there is a full day ahead of me tomorrow."

"You have your sermon ready?"

"David and Bathsheba and forgiveness."

"Glad it is not Ahab and Jezebeel."

"You are a Jezebeel a little bit. Seems you have a power over me no other woman has ever had."

"Not even Sadie?"

"Sadie rules my heart. You rule my emotions."

She caught up with me, and we held hands on our return walk. This time we sloshed along through curling surf close to shore.

"Here's another sand dollar for Sadie," she said wrapping it carefully in tissue. She was one of the few women I ever knew who could leave her purse behind, but she did carry a canvas bag in which she put her finds.

"Here's something even more rare."

"What is it, Hank?"

"A sea crucifix. See, here is Christ on the cross; here is his crown of thorns. On the back are two Roman shields. Here are the Roman eagles."

"How interesting. Where did it come from?" she asked.

"It is a skull out of a sea catfish. Listen, when you shake it you can hear the Roman soldiers' dice."

Mary took it and carefully wrapped it. "Has Sadie ever been down here with you?"

"No. The accident happened before I knew about the Gulf."

"Poor Sadie and poor you. It must have been very hard on both of you, loving each other so much and not being able to be together. I am glad that since it happened, we met. It will not hurt her, my taking care of you for her."

We worked a great deal of our intensity out in our constant lovemaking. Now there was a love that was deeper than anything either of us had felt before.

"Hank?"

"Yes, darling."

"You are sure it will not ruin things, my going to San Francisco with you?"

"Not the way we will work it out. We will fly out on separate planes and meet a day before the convention starts. I will have to be at the convention, but we will be together at night and when I can sneak off from meetings."

"Let me take care of reservations. John and I lived there two years. I will pick a discrete hotel away from town traffic. We will have room service so others will not see us out together."

"It sounds like you went through this before."

"Hank, do not say that. You and John are the only ones I was ever intimate with."

I asked, "How come you came down to meet me that morning?"

"I watched you from a sand dune while you swam. I left before the shark hit you, or I would have helped you."

"Probably best you did not. They might have liked you better. Wish we could drive home together. We'll stop and eat lunch."

"I have a picnic basket all packed. You cannot afford to be seen by a nosy church member. Then I would really be a Jezebeel."

"I will get in with you and leave my vehicle parked at Granbury. You sure it will not be too much trouble to bring me back?"

"Not at all, Hank. We will use my car this time."

"Make those reservations for us to fly together," I said.

"You are sure? There will be others going who will know you."

I said, "We will pretend to have sat together accidentally. It will be hard for me to keep my hands off you, but I can."

"No promises, Hank. At least it will be a night flight."

Her house, if located in Italy, would have been a villa. Located on a high hill, her back door opened out on a steep trail with steps over the roughest parts. Someone had laid railroad ties in interesting ways down to the water far below.

"Beautiful place, Mary."

"It will be lonely."

"I will be able to stop by on my way to school."

"That will be next fall."

"I decided to start work on my thesis this summer."

"You must have an understanding church to let you off so much."

"They wanted me only for my name and the people I can attract. Once crowds quit coming, I am through."

"What will you do then?"

I said, "Move on. With a doctorate, there is always teaching."

"Would you mind?"

"Not at all."

We made leisurely love before Mary drove me back to my camper. Darkness was beginning to close down around us when we drove back in silence. Mary cried occasionally, not hard, but steadily.

"We will have to be careful, Hank."

"Think I will buy a boat and dock it in the Marina down from your house. Church members won't be suspicious of me being there so much."

"Was Sadie all right when you called?"

"Yes, she had a good time with our parents."

"I am glad, Hank. Shall you tell her about us?"

"No, she will know. We will probably never mention it. I will tell her about the Gulf and give her all the things you collected for her. She will be appreciative."

"Perhaps sometime I will meet her."

"It can be arranged. You are going to start coming to our church?"

"Thought I would. It has been so long since I attended."

We rode together in silence until I turned and kissed her before we parted. Everything worked the way we planned it. We were together a great deal even before San Francisco.

"How was Sadie?" she asked me Tuesday when I stopped by after my trip to school to talk over my work for the summer.

"She was elated. Her dad and I went fishing yesterday at Proctor."

"You like her parents, do you not?"

"We grew up together. Guess neither one of us knew which parents belonged to which."

"Anyone question you?"

"Only my mother. She knew."

"How?"

"She said I acted the way my father did after he first married her."

"Do you mind?"

"Not at all."

We were resting from our lovemaking before I had to go back.

"I see why they hired you, Hank."

"Why is that?"

"You are good. I do not think it is make-believe with you. Your sermon Sunday touched me."

"Thank you."

"Believe I will join," Mary said testing my reaction.

"It would explain things better. Members are driving in farther than you."

From that time on, there was never a time that Mary did not undress any time she expected me. She always swept to the door in a flowing red robe that accented her features. Every time I loved her more deeply.

When she found that my favorite color was red, she decorated her room in that color - her bed, curtains and a throw rug on the brown carpet. We often lay in her sunken bathtub together instead of on the bed.

San Francisco is a blur. There was the heady moment when delegates elected me to the presidency of that great denomination. Since the meeting was held in the west, a great number of people attended who had heard me preach. Way in the back was a lady in red and black who I could hardly recognize. It was Mary.

There were some who opposed me, Fundamentalists who had heard about my stand on Evolution were venomous. But there were not enough there to overthrow me, even though some said they tried every dirty trick in the book to keep me from my office.

My inauguration speech was full of forgiveness. I vowed to pull the convention back together.

I pleaded fatigue so Mary and I could spend night hours together. It was a trip full of pleasures. Three times we dared to drive her rented car to an out-of-the-way place where we dined in luxury. Contrary to what a deacon reported later, neither one of us ever had alcoholic beverages with our food.

We spent that summer in a happy dream world. Neither of us thought we were being watched, even though those who testified seemed to know what took place. The trial was three years after that summer. Undoubtedly, those who spied on us did not seek my resignation from the church or from my position of president.

My schedule forced me to do my rodeoing in between times. Even then, my name drew top billing. My riding was more flamboyant. Bull after bull failed to throw me. Mary brought me good luck.

At every event she was seated high in the bleachers overlooking the arena. No longer did I fly with a church member. Using the excuse that my duties as president required me to travel a great deal, I flew with Mary whenever possible.

It was at Huntsville, at the Texas State Prison, where I almost lost my life. When a prison chaplain heard that I needed to interview men who had been converted while in prison, he invited me to hold a two-service revival while I was there.

"You will be perfect, Hank. This is a rodeo-crazy world. You ought to be around here when we hold our prison rodeo."

My work with prisoners was to assist trained mental health workers in gathering data on conversion experiences. Jail house salvations are a dime a dozen. Take a jury, when they hear about how a burglar gave his heart to Jesus and how he wants to witness for Christ, they will try and either get him a suspended sentence or a much shorter stay in the slammer.

Murderers are kept alive by their pleas for their promised change in life-style because Jesus is their co-pilot now. My purpose was to search out and determine how many of these jailhouse conversions were authentic and if they did change personalities.

Through P.A. systems, closed circuit television, and open meetings, my prison preaching seemed to make a tremendous difference to thousands. Men were asking for volunteers to help them overcome their sinful natures. I was far too busy with my research program to do more than advise those ministers who flocked in to help with this important work.

"Hank," my chaplain friend said, "if we could learn to use the Gospel message for behavioral modification in these inmates, we could do something for these people. Instead of keeping them for years and then letting them back into society, we could accomplish something. It would certainly make work easier here."

"Thing is, they can easily fake conversion. Even real converts can regress into their old behavioral patterns too easily." I thought of my double life with Mary. This would have been a clinical example of a dual behavioral pattern made necessary by circumstances. Or was it? Would I have taken up with Mary even if Sadie had been fully functional?

It was my last interview when it happened. His name was Charlie Adams, a product of a broken home and hard drinking. He killed a policeman on a Houston wharf when he was on liberty off a tanker.

There was some extenuating evidence that kept him from the electric chair.

Two burly guards brought him in to the interview room. He should have been in chains, but his drivel about Jesus saving his soul had us all fooled.

If there ever was a converted man, this was he. His conduct and conversation exemplified a Christian man. His demeanor was still that of a rough sailor, but he was kindness and gentleness personified. It was as if Jesus had come down in our midst in the form of this man, who society thought it had killed.

The chaplain and I observed him through a glass while he waited for our interview.

"Warden is getting ready to release him. His stay here seems to have completely rehabilitated him. His lawyer is pushing for early release on grounds that witnesses falsely accused this man."

"How about a lie detector test?"

"Hank, he has passed them all. There is no electronic indication that he ever saw the dead policeman. We gave him Sodium Pentothal. Same results. Nothing."

I asked, "Could he be two complete personalities, one so separated from the other that nothing can reach it?"

"We know little about that aspect of the personality. By the way, your work in getting food supplies started for starving people in Africa is appreciated. You are going to use your position as president for good, are you not?"

"I hope to."

"You ready?" he asked me before we both took a deep breath.

"If you are."

They left us alone so Adams would talk more freely.

"Mr. Adams, Hank is going to ask you some questions about your conversion experience. He is working on a book dealing with how conversion alters human behavioral patterns."

"I am ready, but first let me tell you how the Lord Jesus Christ came into my life and set me free from all my sins. He has given me patience and courage to face this false imprisonment. He has shown me they crucified him on Calvary on false evidence."

"Continue, Mr. Adams," I said when he hesitated.

"It is with humbleness I rejoice that, out of thousands of prisoners in this facility, it has been me who was chosen by my Lord to receive salvation's free gift."

"Can you tell us about your conversion, Mr. Adams?"

My recording machine made a whirring noise, as he continued to speak with great conviction. "All I ever knew in life was being beaten by a drunken father, who drove my mother to an early grave through his sadistic behavior. My only brother died in a drunken stupor before he was twelve years old.

"I shipped out to sea with the U.S. Navy during the Korean conflict. Twice I was placed in the brig for cursing an officer."

"But yet you won the Congressional Medal of Honor?" the chaplain asked.

"Yes. It was a cold, dark night when ten of us went ashore in a small landing boat to destroy an enemy communication system. I was instrumental in helping four of the men return. Even though severely wounded, I continued to fire my M-1, even when I was so badly wounded that I had to tie myself in a firing position."

"Were you a Christian at that time?" I asked.

"No. Far from it. Nor was I when my physical condition caused me to be transferred to a Veterans Hospital. I recovered enough for the service to discharge me."

"Mr. Adams, will you describe your conversion experience?"

He was not quite rational when he told us about a great light shining down upon him, and how a voice came out of the wall telling him that he was God's child.

"And since that time, you possessed an altered personality which has allowed you not only to be an exemplary prisoner, but a witness to others?" I asked.

"Yes sir, that is correct. You are the bull rider who spoke to us?"

"Yes, I am. Why?"

"I wanted to be sure 'cause you are a big enough cheese, you are going to get me out of here."

"What do you mean?" the chaplain asked.

"See this," the prisoner spoke softly. He pulled a semi-automatic from his belt. "It will shoot six times. Enough times to kill both of you. Now, tell the guards to let me out with this bullshitter, Chaplain, or he is a dead man."

"And your wonderful conversion experience?"

"Chaplain, it is not worth a damn! Only thing it was good for was to get me some easy time. Now get that door open before both of you go to hell!"

Prison doors clanged open and shut before and after us, while the two of us made our walk down prison corridors. Adams was brilliant. He was first on one side, and then the other. Never did he stay long enough in one place to let guards get a bead on him without danger of hitting me.

We made our way out to the outer court wall. Prison guards in observation posts turned their rifles on us. Sweat poured down my spine as I marched before this monster, who dug his pistol viciously in my ribs. There was little hope of breaking and running.

We went through prison gates, with electronic devices letting us through.

Out in the parking lot, he ordered a government official out of a state vehicle. Entering the white stationwagon, he motioned for me to climb in the back seat. It was in this one split second that I pretended to trip over a speed breaker. When my body failed to shield this demon, two rifle shots rang out in unison.

My captor never knew what hit him. Two blood-gushing holes at the base of his skull, which a person could cover with a silver dollar, told the story.

"Nice work," a guard said. He dodged in and out from among the parked cars. "You hurt?" he asked, while he checked the dead convict's pulse.

"No, but I will need a little while to stop shaking."

"Understood."

The chaplain came running up. "Hank, what do you think of that conversion experience?"

"It is not worth the tape it is recorded on."

Sadie welcomed me home with fear on her face. "Hank, it looked like it was all over for you. I was so afraid. I do not know what I would do without you here to give me strength."

She did not know that she was the strong one.

My picture was on television for three days. It took newspaper editors another week to forget me. I called Mary from a phone on the courthouse square. It was a mistake. The operator testified at the trial about the call she listened in on.

CHAPTER
THIRTEEN

I had a stack of applications for the job of director of our expanding kindergarten. Not only was our church growing rapidly, but our other facilities needed more workers and more space.

The church-run kindergarten was a new idea that had worked well in larger cities. Bulton was growing, with new industries moving in every day. Only the lack of an adequate water supply for industrial use hampered us from a population and building boom.

Industrialists from cold northern cites wanted to use our natural gas and oil supply. Some came to study our unique church and decided to bring their families and friends. Retired people were stopping here instead of leaving west Texas oil fields and going on south.

There were ten applicantions before me. One from a lady named Peggy, drew my attention. She was from a prominent Fort Worth oil family of multi-millionaires, the old money kind, who had been through the cattle boom.

Her credentials were the best: B.S. in social work, Southern Methodist University; M.S., in Child Development, Baylor; M.R.E. in Child Religious Development, Southern Baptist Seminary.

Stepping to the church secretary's office, I asked them to notify this young lady that she was the one we wanted to talk to at her earliest convenience.

She was in two days later. Kent interviewed her and recommended her highly. Two weeks later, she came to work. It was my first sight of her.

She was a honey blonde, twenty-four, with very pretty legs. The rest of her was all right, also. She introduced herself her first day of work and then got lost in the shuffle.

My jobs kept me busy. We were trying to make some policy changes in the Southern Baptist Convention. We could not be members of the world church family because of our closed church membership, and in some churches, closed communion.

It was my hope that we might at least reach our hand out in friendship to the world church community. Isolating a major group of Christian believers was not, in some of our leaders' minds, the best way of serving the world. Few of us wanted to join the World Council of Churches, but we did want to take more of a leadership role in some of the Baptist world organizations. We were meeting opposition from more conservative groups.

Also, I wanted to involve the denomination in a world peace organization, not the draft card burning groups who were so prominent, but a more moderate group of people, who wanted to discuss ways to prevent war.

We were making strides in trying to overcome world hunger, not by sending food, but by sending experts in food production to underdeveloped countries.

It was not all easy sailing, even with our increased food program. There were those in the convention who loudly protested any type of social gospel. They wanted all monies and efforts spent on converting the heathens instead of feeding them.

It was constantly my duty to fly all over the United States, and sometimes the world, to represent my denomination.

Working on my thesis was also draining my time. In spite of all this, there was only one week that Mary and I did not get together. If she had not been independently wealthy, it would not have worked. She flew to strange cities and took up residency in suites joining mine. She was a great source of relaxation after a hard-won victory over moss-backed church boards members.

Our meetings at her lake home continued. It was only a few minutes' drive off the main highway to Fort Worth. I had two families instead of one.

"You are worse than a Bringham Young Mormon," she said.

"Essentially you have two wives, but no children. When are you going to invite me over to your house so I can meet Sadie? It would seem that we are not strangers anymore. I have read all five of her books. They are delightful."

While I was at Madison Square Garden for the last time, she went to my house and visited Sadie.

Both of them told me about the visit. "She came to talk about my latest book, Hank. She is one of the most gracious ladies I ever met. If I die young, try to marry a lady like her. Promise me, Hank."

Neither of us mentioned my relationship with Mary. Whether Sadie ever knew for sure, I do not know. Neither Mary, as far as I was sure, nor I ever let her know, nor did we try to hurt her in any other way.

Mary was a frequent visitor in our home after that. She never forced herself in, she came only when Sadie invited her, which was often.

We took her mobile home on several trips to isolated places where no one was likely to recognize us. At first I objected to using her equipment, but she said, "Hank, people are not as likely to recognize us together in this as they would in yours."

Our relationship had matured. It had not grown cold, except on winter nights, when we huddled in bed together keeping each other warm with our love.

Once we spent two days together on a hunting lease west of Mason. Mary had planned the trip well. Taking pains to make sure we would be the only hunters on this large ranch, we were at our freest when, once again, we found the old thrill of Padre Island. There was a small river running through the ranch where I caught catfish while Mary picked large bouquets of red and yellow leaves to decorate the church sanctuary.

She came back from her task all sticky and nestled up to me on the riverbank. We made love again out in the open. It was a memorable event.

She sat with me in the deer stand perched up in a tall oak tree. This was one of the few times I used the rifle that I carried in the gun rack of my pickup.

Mary sat teasing me with her hands, when the buck came out of the woods and stood there, looking suspiciously around. It was some bigger than the ones Kent and I had killed that year when I was working off my aggressiveness.

This one stood with his head full of antlers pointed up at me. I took deliberate aim and shot it through the heart so there would be a mountable head. We gutted the carcass together.

That night with Mary was something special. Both of us became savages, each trying to satisfy the other. After a short love session that ended much too soon, we spent the rest of the morning in a continuous act that left both of us relaxed and sleepy.

Next morning we joined the long caravan of deer hunters, who clogged the Texas highways, with displays of hunting trophies tied to the hoods and tops of vehicles.

We were probably seen together by a church member when we stopped to investigate a blazing pickup along the highway. It belonged to an old man who had tried to cook his venison on a kerosene stove, in his camper, while he drove down the road.

We would not have become involved had it not been that the old man was by himself. Three of us fought the fire for over an hour. Finally, we hooked a log chain to his camper and drug it off on the highway.

It was while we were fighting the fire that a familiar voice spoke to me. "Hello, Hank."

I turned to face one of our most faithful members. "You are a long way from home."

"Yes. Used my two days off this week to do a little deer hunting."

"Don't see your rig."

"It is broken down. Flat back off the road."

This little lie took me over half an hour to get out of. I finally told him bluntly that he need not take me back to fix the flat. He drove off, unconvinced.

That warm fall day, Texas woods were ablaze with red oak leaves, yellow cottonwoods and scarlet sumac. There are two times, most years, when Texas turns loose in a riot of color. One is in the spring, when every flower tries to outdo itself in blues, reds, oranges and yellows. The other beautiful time is in early fall, when first frost turns leaves to a fashion plate of fall colors.

Most years, leaves remain green until November before they think seriously about turning. This was one of those long leisurely falls, with a thin layer of smoky haze over the land.

I pulled the mobile traveler over before we reached her home. She had been pestering me with her hands all afternoon. There, in a small roadside park, I gave her what both of us wanted. She could aggravate me the most while we drove down long, lonesome highways. She would come over close and rub me with her hands until I could not stand it any longer. I liked it.

I would have had more trouble with the more conservative members of the convention if this had not been one of those years when church membership increased by over seventy percent in the first half of the year.

By January, a revival had broken out throughout the Baptist world. It was not one of those showy ones, but it was a steady growing one, which spread silently from one church to another. New Baptist churches sprang up, small religious fires broke out, and congregations grew too large for their facilities. Rather than put up larger, more expensive buildings, they built missions in different parts of the cities and towns.

For the first time in many years, Baptist churches in the rural sections of the state blossomed. With a vanishing rural population, most country churches, which had stood in shady groves of giant trees for generations, had closed their doors. Now, some of these rural missions were being revived.

Baptist churches were built in the cities and suburbs faster than they had ever been before. Through my instigation, seminary and college students traveled in church-sponsored planes as far as Canada and Mexico to start missions. A giant came alive that year, and I took pride in my part in it.

Sadie also came alive under Mary's friendship. What those two did for each other, I will never know, but there were always new curtains and pictures throughout the house. At odd times throughout the day, when I ran home for a minute, Mary and some of her other friends would be playing games and laughing with my wife.

Mary knew when Sadie had reached her limit, and she and her friends would leave as quickly as they had come. Sadie seemed to blossom under the new attention the same way I did. This was probably the happiest year of my life. There were so many achievements. Bulton church started missions in over two hundred outlying areas. We were not content to bring people in from other areas and add them to our congregation. Instead, we sent our roots far out into the region around us.

The state organization built a new Baptist Student Center close to the university in our town. The Baptists hired teachers who refreshed students' minds with new ideas, instead of trying to fill them with the same old dull stuff they had heard for years. They explored new concepts in religion that were every bit as exciting as Galileo's discoveries with his telescope.

Best of all, we were able to get state universities to stop fighting with our Baptist Chairs of Religion. We got rid of those who opposed every new idea that might contradict their narrow concepts of Biblical interpretation and hired people who were more broad-minded. It worked.

Even my English professor friend chuckled over our new program. "Hank," he said one morning at the meeting place where we picked up our daily mail, "you let a fresh breeze blow through those Baptist students' minds. Always before, they fought everything we did. There were times when I could not get through a teaching session because a half dozen of them would interrupt any new ideas that were thrown at them. Now, some of them are coming up with new ideas themselves."

"I am glad to hear that. Does this mean you are thinking about becoming a Baptist?"

He harrumphed as he walked on down the sidewalk, with his head held high. Then he turned back to say, "Some of them are actually taking part in the drama department."

"Is that unusual?" I asked.

"Last year, they were pushing actors off the stage."

133

"Maybe your plays have improved."

We laughed together.

The most amazing growth came in the western expansion of the church into ranch country. Students in universities throughout the west started going out and holding services in isolated gathering places. Abandoned schoolhouses came alive, as rural people used them for religious gathering places.

Mary and I talked about the change that was taking place when we celebrated Valentine's Day over a glass of grape juice, in her home, the day after. She insisted I spend the real day with Sadie.

"Hank, it seems like people have caught the spirit of true Christianity instead of a narrow view that no one really cared for. Do you think this will stop with you?"

"I hope not. In fact, it will take something pretty drastic to keep me from being president again next year."

"Like a scandal with me?"

I went over and drew her down on the couch by me. "Like a scandal with you."

My time with Mary was not just a time of sex. But we did have plenty of that between her satin sheets and silk covered spreads. She was all that a man could ever ask for, in bed and out. There were times I completely forgot who and where I was.

The only thing that was real was Mary, and her arms around me telling me she loved me, and that I knew it. Those were the precious moments that kept me going. Her willing body never refused me anything I wanted.

We drove up to Nara Visa one Sunday after church. Snow stretched out from Amarillo to home. It was 'way up in the morning before we pulled in to my old home place.

Mother and Sadie's parents were in Bulton. I wanted Mary to see where my roots were. The vast empty land amazed her. "You had all this land, Hank."

"I still do, Mother and I."

"Who runs it for you?" she asked.

"Sadie's father. Come on in and let's get something to eat. It is cold in here, but I will have a fire going shortly."

"I know, Hank, let's go to bed while the house is warming up."

She was that way. Neither of us could get enough of one another. She was the most loving woman in the world.

Some men do not like that in a woman. One man, an oil field worker, even told me he divorced his wife because she wanted too much. It was not like that with the two of us. One or the other of us was always after it.

We ate and I drove her over the land. A man raised on a piece of this earth can never lose his roots. Somewhere, down in this land, my roots grew with the grama and the bushes. There was a part of me still living in this earth.

Shakespeare touched on it in one of his plays, when he spoke of England and how it was being eaten up by foreign powers.

It seemed that this was true of my land. It seemed that our Presidents were more concerned with our image abroad than they were with what went on here on my land. There were years when it cost more to produce our farm products than we got out of them.

"You asleep, Hank?"

"No, just thinking about this land and how we took it away from the Indians. Now, the Government is trying to take it away from us."

"Your thoughts are deep. How you must miss this land."

It stretched out before us like a giant frosted cake, with snow covering all but a few bare spots, where cattle had brushed the snow away to find the rich grama grass, now hidden. It was one of those days when the sparkling sunlight is colder than the snow it illuminates.

Sadie's dad's cowboys had already caked. There was no one to disturb us on this cold February day, when probably the last big snow of the season lay on the ground.

Down around the water holes there were fresh droppings steaming on top of the cold snow. Cowboys had ridden by and broken holes in the ice, holes that would freeze over again tonight, soon after the sun went down behind the western rise of prairie.

It was a trackless wilderness, reaching out into infinity. This wilderness was no more tracked and charted than was the wilderness I faced, where men inhabited a world with only a few markings along the way. These markings were left by people like Moses, Aristotle, Plato, Christ and others, who left small beacons to guide men's feet, as they struggled through thesr wilderness.

"You are silent today, Hank."

"I do my best thinking here, Mary."

"If you should lose Sadie and come back to this land, and if you want me, I will come."

"You won't come with me to a Baptist parsonage?"

"No, all that religion would smother me. You manage to take the smothering out of a church, but some of your members can spread it back as quickly as you remove it."

"People like Bill North and Sarah Jennings?"

"Especially people like Sarah Jennings."

"The only real person in Bulton is that English professor who is always fighting with me. The rest are all ghosts of the way they think Christ wanted them to be. Seems like they forgot the reason Christ came was to free them from their old selves. Speaking of old selves, what would you want me to do if Sadie dies?"

"What do you mean, Hank?"

"A preacher has to have a wife to take care of him. You know how people would talk about a single preacher."

"Marry you some empty-headed woman. One who could help you advance in your career. Do not tie yourself down with a nobody like me."

"But you are the woman I want, my darling."

"I still will be waiting every time you need me, Hank. There is no man going to satisfy me now that you have been with me. You will come back."

"Only way you will come with me for good is if we live on this ranch?"

"That is right. It does not matter if you are ninety and I am a hundred, I will come here with you."

We drove back that night. All the way I fought a snowstorm into Childress. It was worth showing Mary what I was really like.

CHAPTER
FOURTEEN

Do not get the idea that Sadie and I were never together. Two nights a week were Carmelita's, to do what she pleased. Most times, we had quiet evenings while Sadie wrote and I worked on various projects. Until it was finished and became a best seller, my work on conversion took more time than my sermons.

Most ministers' committees meet themselves to death. The church hired Kent to take care of routine things. Forgetting all paranoid thoughts, the church, at my insistence, gave him a free hand to handle everything but the services. Sometimes, when I was on vacation, he also did that.

The two evenings Sadie and I reserved for ourselves, we had candlelight meals by her bedside. She could feed herself, but she could not manage knives or hold cumbersome water glasses.

Even I forgot how much of an invalid she was. It is hard to remember, with all she achieved with her literary work, that she was severely crippled. It was impossible to take her out of bed. Her many injuries caused her bones to break with any rough treatment.

She made a world out of her bedroom and the patio, in summertime, where we could roll her bed. There was nothing depressing about being with her, in fact, I needed this quiet time with Sadie as much as I needed my time with Mary.

This was the time to talk out my dreams. She gave me expert advice on how to handle things without being bossy. Sometimes, she passed on things she heard so I could adjust my actions in certain situations.

Sarah Jennings was our main source of information. Punctually, at ten o'clock each Tuesday morning, she came to visit with Sadie. Both seemed to enjoy these meetings, and for Sadie, it was a window into what church members were thinking.

"People are talking about how good a job Peggy is doing with the kindergarten, Hank," Sadie told me.

"She is a very capable person. I have only talked to her a time or two, but Kent seems to think that she is very good."

"Now, if you could get something going for those elderly ladies, then you would have it made."

"Like what?" This was a sore spot in our church. Widows with nothing else to do dreamed up gossip and trouble. "If they would get interested in old men and leave the staff alone, it would be all right. But they will not."

"The way these old men die off first, there are not enough to go around."

"They could share," I said, thinking of Sadie and Mary.

"It would not work. What you need to do is hire a director and have weekly activities for people who have nothing else to do."

"Like what?" I asked.

"Quilting. Exercise. Writer's club. You might get by with bridge clubs, but members would probably accept dominos better."

"I guess dancing would be out. Thanks, it might work. There is a lady here who would be just right for the job. It would probably cause trouble bringing in an outsider," I told Sadie.

"I do not know who you have in mind, but have you considered Mary?"

"That was not who I had in mind, but she would be perfect. Do you think she wants to do it?" I asked, wondering if we could work together without getting into trouble.

"She practically begged for the church to consider her. Sometimes you do not hear well."

"It would tie her down."

"Let her direct. Hire a paid worker, but let Mary do the work. She has some good ideas."

While we talked pleasantly over our meal, a draft caused the two candles to dip and flutter shadows across the silverware and white patterned china. It was early spring. The fragrant smell of honey-suckle came through windows. Birds chirped sleepily on the limb outside.

"It will be time for your vacation before we know it. Do you have any special plans for this year?"

"Probably the coast again."

"You like it there, don't you?" Sadie asked.

"My favorite place."

"Tell me about it again, while we eat. You know, I never saw either ocean."

"There is nothing like it anywhere in the world, Sadie. Sand dunes and beaches stretch all around part of this state. If it was not for rivers cutting in, a person could drive the whole coastline of Texas without ever leaving the beach. On a clear day, a person can see out over the water, and by using a little imagination, see the coastline of South America. Sometimes a ship comes sailing and breaks the horizon. Beach combing is my favorite thing to do. Sometimes I find bamboo and coconuts. There is a large bean, hard as a rock, which washes on shore."

"Did the one you plant ever come up?" Sadie asked, for Mary told her how hard I tried to grow the obstinate seed.

"No, I tried everything. They never grow. Sea Bean is what people along the coast call them. No one I have asked has ever gotten them to grow either. Prettiest thing is when little fish gather in the moonlight and seem to dance on their tails."

"Dance on their tails? What have you been drinking on vacation?"

"Nothing, Sadie. They gather in eddies, where river water is saline enough for them and jump out of the water. Perhaps they are trying to get away from bigger fish, or maybe it is a mating dance. There are so many things I do not know about. I just observe them."

She told me, "Sometimes life is that way, my loved one. It is better to just observe instead of always trying to know all about it. You can take the mystery out of living if you know all about everything. Flowers are prettier if you do not think about their purposes. You are too scientific. Always trying to measure things like human emotions. It is good you are that way, but sometimes turn loose and enjoy instead of trying to figure everything out. You started doing that this year more. It is nice."

I bent down and kissed her gently before I cleared the dirty dishes and stacked them in the dishwasher. We did not speak for a long time, until almost bedtime. Then we merely commented on how warm the weather was getting.

Mary organized a retired people's club the next week. She had people, who had been sitting at home staring at four walls, talking and laughing together in mutual endeavors. It was not just fun. Sometimes they worked, folding napkins for family night supper and filling salt shakers. Then, they reached out into the community to sew clothes for needy people.

"You do not know how much good it does me having this job." Mary stopped into my office for a few minutes to make plans for the coming Monday.

"Just do not get involved on our days together."

We spent my spring vacation on Padre Island again. This time it was relaxing and we enjoyed each other more calmly. The Texas coast is never the same. Salt water laps on the beach the same way each year, but old landmarks are gone from year to year and new ones wash in out of the depths.

There was a large, rusty tank where we entered the area for four-wheel drive vehicles only. Like children, we stopped and examined it thoroughly.

Farther on down, a shrimp boat had foundered offshore, about a hundred yards out. Unmolested, it still carried its lines and tackle. Only the expensive navigation equipment and radio were removed. The first thing we did was to swim out to it. We paddled around in the surf, where it swept back and forth over the breaking boat.

Barnacles had already started attaching themselves to the wood and metal. Climbing aboard the broken hull, we swayed back and forth like babies gently rocking in a cradle. Our lovemaking was much more gentle this time.

We spent time exploring the beaches and inland pastures where cattle roamed. We were walking barefoot through salt grass, when all of a sudden, a rattlesnake struck full length at my bare feet. With great skill, I threw my survival knife at its slithering head. Suddenly, there was a spurt of blood, and its head disappeared. After that, we wore shoes.

"Are you tired of me, Hank?"

"What is there to be tired of, Mary? Perhaps you ask because I tire you. It is much easier for you to leave than it is for me."

"You would not say that if you knew how much I love you."

I took her gently in my arms, and turning her face upward, I showed her how much I cared.

We stayed away from civilization for five days. As soon as I got to a phone, I tried calling home. There was no answer. At noon we stopped at Blanco, and I once again tried. Still, no one answered the phone.

Hurrying on in, Mary left me off at my camper, and after transfering my equipment and a hasty good-bye I drove home. There was a note on the door by the black wreath.

"Son," I recognized my mother's handwriting, "Sadie died Thursday. Funeral is Monday at Nara Visa. Hurry."

Unlocking the door, I first called Mary to tell her what had happened. "You go ahead. I will fly up tomorrow," she told me.

Next I called Kent to make arrangements for Sunday services.

The Bulton operator testified that the first person I called, on learning of my wife's death, was Mary.

141

CHAPTER
FIFTEEN

Spring was on New Mexico's land that Sunday morning, when I stepped off the chartered plane that brought me over from Amarillo.

Mother was waiting for me at the edge of the tarmac. I leaned over and kissed her softly. Both of us were crying.

"Sorry to let you learn about her death so harshly. Sadie's parents wanted her body home as soon as possible. Her death upset them awfully."

"I can imagine. What happened?"

"She just slipped away after breakfast." Mother was crying hard now. "She always seemed like a daughter to me. We used to trade off taking care of you two. Doctor thinks it was a massive heart attack. I am so sorry."

We drove across the plains, hardly seeing the lush prairie grass full of wildflowers. Yuccas were blooming this year, their stalks of white blossoms seemed to bear tribute to one of theirs who would never again ride across these vast plains.

I stopped and grieved with Sadie's parents. Then I went home, changed, and drove back over the dirt road to town. There were a few people at the funeral home, but not many.

There were handshakes and few words, while these ranch people scuffed their boots in the sand and tried to tell me how much they hated what had happened. They had known both of us since we were in diapers.

Hurrying on inside, it was more than I could bear to look on her beautiful face now at rest and without pain. People came in and out, and at times, in my grief, it was hard to remember who was there and who was not.

Mother drove Sadie's parents in around sundown. "Come on, Hank, let's get something to eat."

"Mother, I had rather not."

"You going to stay here all night?"

"Funeral director said I could."

"Do not be too hard on yourself, Son. She died easy. Doubt if she knew what hit her. She had the sweetest smile on her face when she went."

After dinner, Sadie's father came in and sat with me for awhile. "Hank, I must apologize to you. It was not your fault that Sadie got all broken up. She wanted to rodeo as much as you did. Wish you would come on home and take care of things. Age is creeping up on me."

"I cannot do it now. Let's see how things go for a few years."

I walked him back to the car. A crowd stood outside. Ranch people, they dressed in suits that were seldom worn. Their long-sleeved shirts hung down a little below their suit coat sleeves.

They fell back and let us come on through. "That is Hank," a woman whispered. "My, he has grown. Hear he is a big preacher down in Texas. Rodeo star."

I shook a few hands and went on back in. It was as if Sadie and I communicated that night. In my tiredness, she seemed to breathe under the small white fluorescent bulb. Her white face matched the wreath of lillies that hung on the stand next to her.

Next morning, early, I walked across the road and picked wildflowers, which I knew she would appreciate more than these things from a florist's shop. Like candelabra, I put two giant yuccas, one at her feet and one at her head. She looked more natural that way.

Mary came in late that evening and stayed with me for awhile at the funeral home. "Hank, I know you love her. Do not let what happened with us cause you a lot of guilt. The two of us talked it over one day. Sadie knew all about us. She was just glad you were not off by yourself."

"She knew?" I asked.

"I thought it was best. She was so happy for you. She really loved you, Hank. She was always so sorry she could not give herself to you. Said she kept herself for marriage and then was not able to be with you. It hurt her. She was a fine woman, Hank."

"I know it, Mary. You are another one."

We sat quietly apart on the couch, neither of us wanting to touch the other in her presence. People kept drifting in and out. Mother came in to take Mary home. Then they locked the doors.

That second night with her brought back all the memories of spring days and horseback rides. It seemed as if our lives flashed before my eyes. Not sad things. Happy things we did together. She came to me for one last time, and I thought of our times in Colorado's mountains. Then I slept, with my head drooping down into my lap.

Mother and Mary came back in when sunlight touched the windowpane. I said one last goodbye and went home with them to clean up, so we could return for the morning service at the Baptist Church.

Our professor from Eastern was there to hold the services. People from all over had sent messages of condolence. There was a church crowd from Bulton there with me. Friends of ours at Eastern had flown in during the previous day and night.

There was sobbing all through the church. Some of it was soft, but some of it was wrenching. It made me sad to hear how much some of those people grieved. I sat between my mother and Sadie's mother. Their black hats and veils kept getting in the way of their handkerchiefs. Mary sat with the rest of the mourners out in the church pews. She was gone when I looked for her after the funeral.

We rode out to the graveyard, bouncing over the rough, graveled road. I guess death hit me hardest when I saw that mound of fresh dirt with all those flowers banked round. It was almost more than I could bear.

They buried her next to father, under a double tombstone with my name on the other side. Date of birth was there, but the date of death was blank on my side.

I knew it was all over when they started throwing dirt into the freshly dug hole. Sadie had come home at last.

Mother and I spent two days together before I had to fly back. Sadie's dad and I rode out together early the second morning.

"Thanks for not deserting her after she got hurt, Hank. Some men would have."

"She was a wonderful person."

"She was, Son. Her mother and I will always think of you as one of our family, like we always have. None of my business, but are you planning on marrying that woman who came out and stayed with your mother?"

"Mary will not have me, Dad. Said she will not marry me long as I am a preacher. Said she would marry me if I ever come up here and ranch. She is sure she is not cut out to be a preacher's wife."

"Hank, you are doing a wonderful job, but I think you are going to find you are not cut out to be a preacher. Bring her and come back when you are through."

"Put a lot of time in it, Dad. Can't hardly back out now."

"Some things a man can do so long, Hank, then he has to do something else. We are still planning on your taking over both places."

Mary met me at Love Field in Dallas. I had called her and told her that I needed a long talk. "Thanks for coming. It meant a lot having you there."

There was a sadness depressing my thoughts so much that it was all I could do to keep from crying. Intermingled with grief was guilt. I had gone off and left her to face death alone. She would not have blamed me, though.

I kept telling myself over and over that she would have wanted me to go on vacation. After what Mary had told me, if she had not told me just to make me feel better, I felt relieved that she had known. She should have heard it from me.

It was a psychosis I was going through, brought on as much by fatigue as by grief.

"How long has it been since you slept, Hank?"

"Lost track of time."

"You are coming home with me," Mary said.

"I have to leave for Atlanta tomorrow afternoon."

"I do not care. You will have plenty of time."

"Should really check in on the church."

"Kent's handling things."

We drove the hundred miles in silence. Sometimes I could hear Sadie's voice when we drove through wooded areas, then across a bald prairie, and then down along the river.

"I must get home, Mary."

"Come in for a minute and have a hot cup of coffee."

Something she put in the coffee did it. I never asked her what it was, but when I woke up at three o'clock the next morning, she had undressed me and covered me up on her den couch. She was asleep at the end of the couch with my head in her lap.

"Mary," I said gently, "let's go to bed. You must be worn out."

"At least you slept."

We did not touch each other before I left, except when I kissed her at the airport. There was still a numbness from my neck up.

The Atlanta meeting was my most brilliant piece of work. We were trying to give Baptist seminaries more academic freedom. The president of the Southern Baptist Seminary in Louisville was in the hot seat for allowing professors to teach form criticism, which allowed their students to examine the validity of the Biblical writings.

"You are tearing down the basic structure of our faith, the Bible," a white-haired preacher from Dallas shouted.

"We are getting to the bedrock of our faith by examining how and when our Bible came into being," I explained, as if he were a small child.

This made my attacker furious. "Best thing for you to do is tell these students of God's Word that God dictated the Bible in its entirety, verbally, without one dotted i out of place."

"Just like he dictated those Baptist histories and changed P's to B's so it would look like the Baptist Church went back to Christ's time?" I asked quietly.

Things got hot in the meeting room after that. They flung out charges of heresy and some worse utterances. There were press present. Flashbulbs were popping.

The pastor of the First Baptist Church in Dallas yelled, "We should cut off all funds to you atheists in Louisville."

"We are going to teach the truth. Christianity that is based on lies and deception cannot stand. Let's get rid of sand and stand on solid rock," the stern looking seminary president said. "There is no longer any use in deceiving people. It does not make our denomination stronger to stand up for antiquated lies, when the scholarly world is finding that the Biblical text has been contaminated."

The attacker stood. Pointing his finger at the offending seminary professor, he spoke like a prophet of God. "You are a blasphemer. Get you behind me, Satan."

I stepped in. Turning to the gray-haired man from Dallas, I asked, "Do you believe what you are teaching?"

"What do you mean?"

"You did your seminary training in Louisville in an age when the minute examination of Biblical text was even more stringent than it is now."

He looked at me, "Of course, I do not believe that the Bible has come down to us verbatim from earliest times, but we have millions of people out there who need something to believe in. If we start questioning and finding mistakes in the Biblical text, then we are going to destroy their faith."

"Was your faith destroyed by a critical examination of the Scriptures?" I asked.

"No, critical study made my faith stronger," he shouted.

"Why won't it do the same for these people who come to our churches?"

"They do not have the strength of belief that we do. We will shake their faith and they will stop coming to our churches."

"Is faith that never questions of any count?" He paused to let me continue. "Don't you think the basic truths of the Bible are powerful enough to overcome textual criticism? Don't you think the educated layman's faith in God is strong enough for him or her to make a judgment call on the validity of evolution without losing their faith altogether?"

"You are a heretic, Hank," he said, in a voice that doubted.

"We are the ones who are causing people's faith to waiver when we suppress the truth," I continued to reason.

"Do you think that Godless state university professors expounding the lies of evolution and Communism are good for our students?"

"As long as they present both sides, it is all they can do," I said, with some reservations. Sometimes, the Biblical account of creation was ignored in state schools.

"What do you mean, `It is all they can do?' How you ever got to be president of this convention, I will never know. You are an atheist!"

Losing my temper would tear this meeting wide open. Taking a stern stand, I said directly to him, "We cannot censor people's thinking. We cannot sit in every history class and political science class and tell free men what to say."

"How are we going to fight it, Hank?"

"By teaching the truth. That is what we are going to do. The truth shall make us free. We cannot stop the spread of Communism unless we can counter it with a stronger doctrine than theirs."

I had his attention now. "Explain yourself."

"If the free world can stop wars and feed and clothe people, and most of all, allow them to develop into proud, responsible citizens, then we can stop the spread of this red tide. We can not stop it with half-truths and lies."

He was silent.

"Is it not better to teach that we do not know how God created the world, but we believe He did it, than let our best minds study theories? Perhaps some of these evolution theorists can stop the spread of diseases and bad genetics by finding out that all creatures have the same inherent strengths and weaknesses."

Argument did not convince either side, but we did talk. Perhaps I could have done more if it had not been for Peggy and my drive for power.

CHAPTER
SIXTEEN

W hen I look back on what happened, it seems so unreal. It would seem that since my affair with Mary had gone undetected this long, and now that Sadie was dead, I was home free.

Some said, after the trial, it was justice catching up with me. They said Sadie's ghost engineered the whole thing to punish me for what I did to her. It was a gigantic miscarriage of justice. That is all.

Mary and I went through a period of grief for Sadie when we did not touch each other at all. We continued to see each other. We could be a little more open about letting church members see us together, but until we gave a reasonable amount of time for respect for the dead, protocol prohibited what we could do openly.

I sometimes stayed at her house for more than a week at a time. Afterwards, I would come to my cold home, where Carmelita and her children lived and kept things in excellent order.

"Hank," Mary said one morning in late summer, "you must get yourself in hand."

"What do you mean, Mary? It seems everything is working out the way I planned it. I am way past where I should be in my doctorate work. My presidency is secure for another year. The church in Bulton is growing faster than it ever has."

"You are depressed," she told me.

"Isn't that natural? After all Sadie and I were childhood sweethearts."

"Your depression is not over losing Sadie, your depression is over guilt feelings you have over our affair. You have not fished. Hank, worst of all, you have not one single time completed a sex act with me since the funeral. What few times you tried, you gave up in the middle of the whole thing."

"I cannot keep it up, Mary."

"I have noticed. Depression can do that. Why don't you talk to your psychiatrist friend? Maybe he can help."

"I will have to make an appointment. We do not see each other since our joint project is over. A medical doctor said it is fatigue and grief with some guilt thrown in. He did not want me forcing myself. He said it is going to take time."

"You are using me for a crutch. I want you to treat me like a woman instead of a sounding board."

"Marry me. I can arrange it."

"Hank, you know my terms for marriage. You are not going to put me in a goldfish bowl for every church member to examine me with a microscope."

"Sadie never complained."

"Sadie was more church oriented than I am. Besides, she was able to live an almost perfect life in the eyes of the church. She was not able to get up and cause trouble. Isn't that what the church wants for a minister's wife? A paralyzed woman?"

"They criticized us for her card games."

"That is different. I am older than you. That will cause trouble. I am not conventional. One of those old biddies gets after me for painting my fingernails, I will tell her where to go."

"You are outspoken. What do you think is best?"

"Go to a psychiatrist. Look around for another woman," she told me.

"You do not care?"

She tried not to cry, but she did. She cried so hard she got my white shirt and tie all wet. She seemed to never stop crying even after we went to bed together. "Hank, it is not fair for either of us. Find you someone else."

I looked up the psychiatrist. "Hank, you remember what I told you? That you would blow to pieces if everything was not just right for you? You are coming to pieces."

"What do you mean, Doc?"

"Mary is right. You are feeding a depression on your guilt. I do not think it is best to put you under a long-term mental health treatment. It would only hurt you. I certainly do not want to medicate you. You have too brilliant a mind to dull it with tranquilizers. Let's face it, you and Mary are not going to work anything out unless you go back to ranching. You have achieved all you are going to do with Bulton. Both of you have outgrown a bull rider type ministry. Try something different, why don't you? Is there another church that interests you?" I knew the doctor pretended to study notes while he waited for my answer.

"Yes, there is a more liberal church here in Fort Worth that I am interested in."

"Think about trying to get it. A new challenge might snap you out of it."

When Peggy came into my office and talked to me about her job, it seemed it was an answer to my prayers.

"I feel I have done about all I can here in Bulton. These people are narrow. There is really little I can do in educating these children without drawing down a great deal of criticism," she told me.

"What do you mean?" I asked.

"I tried to teach a simple unit on prehistoric creatures. One of the parents objected so much, I had to stop."

"Do you think you could do better somewhere else?"

She named the church in Fort Worth I was interested in. We talked together about the situation for an hour. We went to lunch together.

"Hank, my father can do things for you."

"Like what?"

"With his money he can get you any church in Texas."

Within a month we married. Within two months we had moved into the parsonage in Fort Worth. It seemed like a gigantic dream.

Mary and I talked it over at her house before the wedding. "Hank, I am happy for you, but it is tearing my heart out. I am afraid you are riding for a big fall. You are not a preacher."

"What am I?"

"You are an outdoors man. You belong on a horse. Not a bucking one, either."

"What do you think of Peggy?" I asked.

"She is no Sadie. She will scratch your eyes out, and sic her daddy on you if you ever get out of line. You will be ruined if she ever finds out about me. You can come here and visit, I want you to, but we can never be lovers again." Mary fought for control and lost.

"Oh Hank, I hate to give you up. You mean so much to me. I don't know what I will do without you. Sometimes I wish I had run down the beach as hard as I could when I saw you. It is my fault, but I am hurt."

"You could still marry me."

"It would not work. We would both be miserable."

We talked on the phone after that, but only twice did I go back to see her until after the trial. Then it was not for sexual reasons.

Peggy was still a virgin. In fact, she had seldom gone out with a man. Her schooling and her job had taken most of her time.

We married in the church I was to pastor. There was no expense spared for the wedding. We stood in front of the congregation in regal clothing. It was a formal affair, where men wore tuxedos and women wore formal evening dresses.

Mary attended dressed in an elegant red gown.

You should have seen the pictures of us standing at the front of the church in our wedding attire. Peggy wore a wedding dress with an elegant veil that reached at least ten feet down the aisle. She was the most beautiful bride I ever saw.

When it came time for me to kiss her, it was like kissing a princess.

Champagne was served at the reception, held in Fort Worth's most elegant room. Over two thousand of the city's most acceptable people were there.

Mother flew down for the wedding. She did not look at all out of place, except her hands were rough from ranch work. She was reserved with me. "Hank, I am happy if you are, but somehow I do not think this is what you are going to be happy with."

"What do you mean, Mother?"

"I am not sure you can fit into this mold. Do not kill yourself trying to reshape yourself. I never believed in divorce, but you are getting yourself into something you cannot live in."

"Maybe you are wrong, Mother. Peggy is beautiful."

"She is a lovely girl, and I love her. Please do not wreck both your lives."

We flew to New York City for our honeymoon. Her father reserved a whole suite of rooms in the Waldorf Astoria. I will not describe our sex life, but after Mary, it was not adequate. She did try. You can see how hard when I tell you she was pregnant within a month.

It was a new world for me. I traded my western clothes for tuxedos and a high hat. It was a round of operas and ballets. There were dances and banquets. Somehow I made it, but I never was at ease.

Do not get the impression I was a country bumpkin. In fact, the opposite was true. We were caught up in a whirl that never stopped. There was a constant supply of champagne and fancy food.

These people's religion seemed so superficial it shocked me. Sometimes I wished for Bulton and its narrow ways. Here, I did not even have my friend the English teacher to stimulate my mind. These people were stuffed shirts who lived a luxurious life until they grew senile, and then they sat and counted their stocks and bonds, empty creatures without substance.

"Hank, sometimes I do not think you are happy with your job here."

"Does it show, Peggy?"

"Not in your work. Your sermons are brilliant. It's the way you mope around. Seems like sometimes you are still in Bulton, or at Nara Visa herding cattle."

"It is a change, Peggy. I am where I have wanted to be, or where I thought I wanted to be. Every job's the same. A man wants to get to the top. President of the college, chairman of the board, then from the top, jobs down along the line look better. From here, being back in some rough and tumble job in a cattle town looks better than being stuck in a black robe on Sunday morning, especially if that robe does not have a doctor's markings on it yet."

"It will after May, when you graduate. I did not know if you would be happy here. I liked your style since the day I first met you.

Infatuation, love, call it what you want," she told me.

There was a certain reserve between us. I could not walk over and take her in my arms with the same freedom I had with Mary. It seemed there was always a wall between us, a wall that neither of us could work around. It was as though we had made a business arrangement that neither of us could break.

She came into my office first after accepting the job of director of kindergarten. She came in a second time applying to be my wife. I accepted both applications as work contracts without setting out any stipulations for her to fulfill the second time.

"It will work out, Peggy," I told her. "We will learn how to treat each other." Going over to her, I planned to draw her to me. She pulled away. The wall was still there, only this time she kept it in place.

She came to me in my office the second month of our marriage. It was done very formal. The appointment was set through my secretary.

"Hank," she said after we had gone through our preliminaries, "I am bored. There is a need for a coordinator of your educational work here."

"We have an educational minister who is handling things quite well. What did you have in mind?"

"Creation of a non-paying job which would give me power to make guidelines for an educational program for this church."

"I thought we had such a program," I was dubious about where this was leading. No church will put up with a preacher's wife who tries to run things.

"You have short-term goals set. What I am talking about is an education program designed to educate the person from cradle until at least twenty-one. Perhaps we can extend it on into adulthood."

"Explain yourself better, Peggy, so I can present it to the deacons."

"Of course. Perhaps it would be best to have your educational staff in on this."

"We will have to bring them in if we decide to go ahead with it. Outline what you have in mind."

"Sunday Schools are the most haphazard things on earth, with little rhyme or reason. I not only want to set up a systematic program for a coordinated classroom teaching situation, but I want to help set up the curriculum for the school."

"You mean, write some of the material?"

"Myself and others. We have a church full of educators here," she said.

"Yes. We do seem to attract the cream of the college and elementary teachers. This is interesting. Proceed."

"After we have the educational material ready, then I plan on coordinating a workable program whereby we present different educational material each year of a church member's life."

"Like in a college or seminary?" I asked.

"Exactly. The average church member has no more concept of the total picture than a man in the moon would. Some only know a whale swallowed Jonah, but they have no concept of the reason why it swallowed him. We have people raised in Sunday School who are as ignorant of church teachings as a cannibal on some South Sea Island."

"That is the reason the Southern Baptist Convention and most other religious bodies are in such a mess. They use the Bible for a good luck omen and not for a book with general outlines of how a person should believe," I supported her point.

"Hank, that is what I wish to accomplish. Through the use of education, I want to help people so that by the time they have reached the age where they can reason maturely, they will have some facts on which to base their reasoning."

I said, "most ministers' wives are used in a church only for an ornament and nothing else. Let's see how you do with this."

She presented a course of affirmative action to the deacons and the educational staff of our church that was stupendous. Members voted it into being immediately. In two months, the plan became so fully ingrained in the church that it was running itself without Peggy's help at all.

Instead of preaching sermons on selfish lives, sermons most of our members needed, my sermons concerned inter-personal relationships among the church members and the community.

In the short time I was there, we made some noticeable changes in the way the church members related to the community and to each other.

Community action is the only way to determine the effectiveness of a church's program. I do not mean by how vigorously a church tries to take pornography out of grocery stores, either. It is how much of a Christ-like spirit church members show towards the real world.

It was my purpose to try to turn a self-centered church outward, into the community. Some of these people were dealing with people from all over the world.

Oil was the magic word among our congregation's members. Their roots were in Saudi Arabia, as well as in my native state of New Mexico. With such a cartel of business people, it was easy to see how our church could help shape world thinking.

If only I had had more time.

CHAPTER
SEVENTEEN

Living with Peggy was like living with a complete stranger. She was in love with my image, but she did not give a good old New Mexico hill of beans for me as a person.

In fact, her father told me one of the few times we ever talked that Peggy had wanted to be a minister from the time she could talk. She preached to rows of empty chairs when she was almost too small to stand up in the middle of their huge, carpeted dining hall.

Her parents lived in lavish surroundings. You have heard of Texas millionaires. They passed that stage when her grandfather hit his third oil well on some land in west Texas. Some of these early Texans had old Spanish land grants, and others received large parcels of land after the Mexican War. They were dirt poor until they hit oil.

Peggy's parents were like the Texas longhorn, rough and thick-hided. They got it into their heads that things were going to be a certain way, and that is the way they were. We were married only ten months, but the three of them made some major decisions that were really mine to make.

"Hank, we are going to call our baby, if it is a boy, William Edward, or if it is a girl, Frances Matilda."

"Where did you come up with those God-awful names?"

"Mother and Father chose them for us."

"Don't you think that is our choice to make?"

"Both of them have done so much for you, it should not matter," she said haughtily.

"Done so much for me?"

"In case you do not know it, they got you this church."

"A package deal, was it? Marry our daughter, we will give you one of Texas's finest churches?"

She spat out, "You know, this is the first time this church has hired a Southwestern Seminary graduate? They went back east—Yale, Harvard, a few from Kentucky. It would have been impossible for you to preach here with a degree from Eastern New Mexico. Who ever heard of that quaint little place?"

Soon afterwards, I started going fishing again on my day off, not both days, but the old routine Sunday night trip down to Granbury, where I still had my boat tied up close to Mary's.

We started seeing each other again. There was not anything going on between us, just some visiting back and forth. She was glad to see me the first day I drove down. It was really too cold for fishing. If I remember right, there was snow on the ground.

Some of us had been going down to the power plant, through the icy water and catching fish in the warm cooling water from the generator. I did not risk a dunking in icy water that trip, nor did I stay in Mary's house. I parked my camper a good five miles from her house, alongside a fishing pier.

When the sun came out the next morning, I got out and cast a few times. There was some good action, even in the cold weather. That day, I brought in one of the biggest bass I ever caught.

He hit a hula skirt with bacon rind. I cast back and forth under a giant willow tree that stood bare against the melting snow. Most times snow does not last long in Texas around Fort Worth. Never more than a week, usually a day or two. This one was going fast.

A bass hit hard on my third cast. He came out from under a root and snagged my bait like he was hungry. My pole bent double, and you could have heard my reel singing for a mile on that cold morning.

The only reason I stopped to see Mary was that in cleaning the fish, I stuck my knife through my thumb. It was not an especially dangerous wound, but it bled for an hour.

Soon as I stopped out in front, I kind of half wished I had not. The other half of me was glad I had. It was one of those situations that makes your heart beat about ten times faster than it should. It even made me hope no one was home.

"Come in, Hank. It is so good to see you. I had 'bout given up on you. Thought maybe Peggy is a better woman than I am."

She stopped my flow of blood and bandaged me up.

When she got close to me, it tore me up. "Sit down and I will fix you some coffee. When is the baby due?"

"Sometime in the next two months."

"Guess since you took care of Peggy, you will come see me again." Her eyes twinkled with her teasing.

"No. Town life got to me. Had to get out again."

"I understand. You did not go out in that boat in this kind of weather?"

"No. Did some casting off the pier. Caught a ten pound striper."

"Man drowned here last month going down to the power plant. Person cannot hang on long in this icy water. Be sure and wear a good lifejacket if you take that boat out. It would not hurt you to carry a flare gun."

I could tell she still cared a great deal for me. It showed in her eyes every time she looked at me.

"Cannot stay long this time, Mary, but I will stop by next week."

She kissed me full on my mouth when I told her good-bye at the door. It was one of those kisses where a woman puts her body up against you and presses hard, the kind that makes a person tingle all over, especially where it counts.

It might have blown into another affair if the race issue had not escalated. Authorities had already integrated Mississippi State when it happened. A Negro was lynched in Fort Worth, even before police proved he molested a white woman. In fact, there was never any decisive evidence that he was the one who did it.

A white crowd went into one of those government housing projects that was all black and pulled this man out. It was almost as though they said, "You are black, we are going to take care of you."

What brought it to a head was that I made a one minute speech about God not wanting Christians to judge others, and for us not to take the law in our own hands. It was only a side remark made during the first of my sermon.

It was like I committed adultery up in the pulpit on Sunday morning. Peggy and I barely got in the door when our phone started ringing.

"Hank, we are going to have to get away from here 'till this dies down," Peggy said. "There is not likely to be any trouble from our people, but those people who watch sermons on television can cause plenty of it."

"I am not letting anyone make me leave town, Peggy. This is my home and my church. Until they relieve me of my duties, I am staying."

"Hank, how many black people did you have in Nara Visa?"

"Cook down at the cafe."

"How many were going to Eastern?" she asked.

"Ten or twelve, then. They have let a bunch in since. In fact, when I was there, black people had to stay in Roswell and drive back and forth."

"We are outnumbered here. Let these black people loose, they will take over," she told me.

"They should not bother us here."

"This is liable be the first place they will hit. Seems like they hate us rich white people. We were in Cincinnati when they tore that city up in a riot. First place they hit was a symbol of wealth, they completely demolished the Cadillac dealership and left some of the less prestigious places standing. We do not try to keep colored people in their place because we hate them, it is because they are liable to hurt us," Peggy explained to me.

"Does seem strange they have to live in shacks and government housing when so many of white people live in decent places," I said.

"There is no way you can change the way people think. It looks like the federal government is going to step in and do away with some of this discrimination. They can do it. You cannot. All you will do is make people hate you if you try."

It was three weeks before I felt it was safe enough to leave Peggy, although Carmelita and her family had moved in with us. Our parsonage had a servant's house that was nicer than the house I was raised in.

One thing you could say about my Fort Worth church, ask for money for a worthy cause, and you got it. We did some real nice things with Boy's Clubs and mission stations in the downtown area. Our church was supporting soup kitchens and welfare missions. There was not a stingy person in the church. A number of them were also doing volunteer work downtown without letting anyone know it. Some did their work through the Kiwanis and Lion's Clubs, but a number of them did their good through the church.

Time did not drag on my hands even though my rodeoing was over. This was also my last year as president of the convention. There were a number of loose ends to tie up. There had not been a spectacular change in the working of the denomination, but people were beginning to wake up. Letters came every day asking me to stay on for another year, but I believed another person would bring in fresh ideas.

"Are you going to do your work with western missions this summer, Hank?" Peggy and I were talking quietly at the breakfast table.

"Why?" I asked.

"I was wondering how much to count on your help with the new baby."

"I will be around enough, but I am planning on starting back into missions. This church has taken a lot out of me."

"Guess this is different from Bulton, isn't it?"

"Not really. People have their same old prejudices, they have enough money to hide them here," I said.

We started talking about our baby. Peggy came over and I made it kick by rubbing it a little. "It is going to be a boy."

"How can you tell, Hank?"

"By the way he kicks. I can tell he is going to be a bull rider for sure. Probably be a good quarterback, but with that kick, he might be a place kicker. Cowboys needed one this past year."

"Hank, I know it is going to be a girl."

"How did you figure that out?"

"Way she twists around. Boy could not do things she does."

We were having some real tender moments with this child. It

looked like the baby would draw us together when nothing else could. It bothered me that Peggy always pulled away after I caressed our unborn baby for a moment.

I had given up on ever having a child. There had not been a chance with Sadie. Mary was incapable, but it was hard to give her up completely. However, it looked like Peggy's and my marriage was finally going to work.

In spite of our baby, Peggy was still working with the Sunday School. It had been a hard job changing the old ideas, where teachers gave gold and silver stars to children who knew the memory verse and brought their Bibles.

She was not trying to do away with all the old, but enough of it to make things work for the individual a little more. Kind of thing my English professor friend had been trying to do with students. Let them be themselves a little more, rather than being little houses all in a row with the same kinds of windows and doors. There was a popular song about that. It always made me think of Peggy.

Every Sunday, I walked down the corridor when children came into the church. It was my reward to see little girls skipping down long halls with little boys, all dressed up in fancy suits, following after them. Some of the boys had already dirtied the knees of their well-pressed suits.

We had some of those children who would make it into Who's Who lists in a few years. Some of our high school children were leaders in their schools. The ones who excelled were our college young people. Most of them were going out of town, but those who stayed and brought their friends were people to be proud to have.

It was here my interest lay. Older people had pretty well made up their minds what they were going to do. These bright, young minds were a challenge. They did not call me by my first name, but they were always friendly and interested. Any time one would speak in the pulpit, I always made time. These were beginning to be my people, like those in Bulton had been. It had taken awhile, but it was worth it. We were growing on each other.

Christmas had been a special time, with so many college students home for the holiday. We had a church full of parents watching their angels and shepherds lead Mary around. The part that was especially touching was when the little lambs came in dressed in white, woolly fleeces and gathered around the Christmas tree.

It was still winter when I last preached in the church, but bushes were starting to burst into bloom. There were even a few bees out buzzing around in the chill air. Some of the ladies were starting to put away their heavy winter clothes and wear lighter garments. Spring came early in Fort Worth.

That last Sunday, I started watching pink and blue clad babies and wondering if Peggy's and mine would be that big. I noticed how much Peggy was showing. It would have hurt her if she knew I thought of Sadie and the expecting mother cows, but it did go through my mind. Peggy would not have understood.

CHAPTER
EIGHTEEN

Now that it is all over, I should have recognized signs of insanity in Peggy. With all my training and study, those telltale signs that point to one who is on the verge of cracking up went unnoticed.

Mary came into church that Sunday evening. She and Peggy knew each other, but they had never been particularly good friends in Bulton. Peggy had been over to see Sadie when Mary was there. As far as I have been able to find out, Peggy never knew about Mary's and my special arrangement. As far as that went, I did not realize anyone, except possibly my mother, knew.

Sunday evening services were quite informal. Unlike Bulton, there was no hard-sale evangelism desired or expected. In spite of this, about as many joined the Fort Worth church while I was there as did the Bulton church. Baptist ministers are sticklers on numbers. Some are so paranoid, they have counters designated to put down how many women and how many men, what age people, estimated salary - those kinds of things. I was no exception.

From the pulpit, Mary's black pillbox hat offset her red suit trimmed in black fur. All kinds of memories went through my mind that evening, while I brought the sermon. Some said it was my most brilliant. But my mind was on Padre Island, with an attractive woman who had given me all I ever wanted.

It is funny with me, or was, when I was preaching, my mind did all kinds of strange things. That evening it undressed Mary and laid her down on the sand in a thousand different ways. After I said the last Amen, it was my customary habit to take up my place at the rear entrance to the sanctuary and shake hands with those present.

All went well. "How are you?" "So nice to see you." "You must come back more often." It was a pleasant chore greeting the faithful and the unfaithful.

When I thought all were accounted for and properly told good night, back in the sanctuary Mary and Peggy were quietly visiting. Not wishing to seem rude, I started to tiptoe back to where my hat and coat were behind the choir.

"Oh Hank," Mary said.

"So good to see you, Mary. You will have to do this more often." What would have been more truthful would have been, "I miss you so much, Mary. It would be so nice if the two of us could slip away for even an hour."

She brought me out of my daydreaming. "Peggy, excuse me, I need to speak to Hank a moment."

All she told me was that she had noticed that my boat had water in it and needed to be bailed out before it sank. She passed her message quietly. Apparently, Peggy did not hear what we said.

"Thank you for telling me, Mary. I will be down tomorrow to take care of things."

"Stop by a moment when you come," she said. I am sure Peggy heard.

"Since we are expecting, I am afraid to leave the house at night, or I would come down tonight and take care of things." We laughed when we parted with a lingering handshake, which would have looked like a sign of affection to others. It stirred my blood when her body pressed me for a moment and then was gone.

Peggy said, "I bet you are tired, Hank. It is too bad you have had to give up your night campout after Sunday service. It seemed to relax you so much."

"I will start taking my son pretty soon."

"It is your daughter, and she will not be running around all over this state at night fishing." There seemed to be no anger or suspicion in her eyes when we gathered up my things and drove off home.

Slipping out of bed next morning, I backed the pickup quietly after making sure everything was in the back toolbox for fishing.

Now that I think about it, the rifle was missing from its customary rack over the back window. It could not have been there.

It was a thirty minute drive to Mary's house. She gave me black coffee. "A moment Hank, and I will throw on something and go with you." A deacon testified we spent time together that morning, time enough to have had sexual relations. There is no use pressing the point that we did not, even though I wanted to more than once that day.

It was a quick task bailing out the boat and then we took it across the lake to check out the motor. It was one of those powerful ones used for water skiing in summer. Although I had never used it for that purpose, it was fully capable of pulling two people without throttling the motor down at all. It was not an ideal fishing boat, but the price had been good.

"Hank, it is so good to be out with you again. I can live the rest of my life on our memories," Mary told me.

"Ever sorry you made the decision you did?"

"Every day, Hank. But when I see you and Peggy together, I am glad. Now you will have a family. To think you are about to become a father. I will bet you never had any more fun making it than we did trying. I kept hoping doctors were wrong and that you would make me pregnant sometime. Hank, you would have had to marry me then."

"What would you have done about Sadie?"

"I would have kept my little wood colt a secret until you were free. It never happened." She brushed a tear out of her eye, and I held her close for a long time. How anyone saw us out in the middle of the lake, I do not know, but a fisherman testified at the trial that we had been very intimate that day.

It was a little after noon when we docked. "Wish I could stay longer, Mary, but Peggy might need me." She rode back to her house with me and insisted I have a sandwich before leaving. It was so good to be back in her house for a short time. Memories kept hitting me. She would have gone to bed with me if I'd asked, but that would not have been fair to Peggy and our unborn child.

She kissed me at the door again. Softly but long and lingering. God!

"Good-bye, Hank, I will be up one day to see the baby."

"I hope you will."

Piecing together what people told me and from testimony at the trial, Peggy must have followed me that morning. She had seen Mary and I together. Perhaps she saw us embrace. It hurts me to think she did. She had no business driving her car in her condition.

She had not lingered long at the lake. It must have taken her at least an hour to fix the gun the way she wanted it. It takes time to figure out what she did.

You do not just tie a strong cord to a trigger and fire a gun. Think about it. If a gun barrel is pointed at you, it has to be with the trigger so it cannot be pulled except by a backward leverage that pulls it.

She must have done it by herself. You will understand why, I know, before this is over.

Still, after all this time, the memory haunts me. Perhaps over the years, the memory will fade away, but it will never leave.

Peggy opened the front door just before I arrived home, and my rifle shot her fully in the stomach, directly through our unborn baby. It was a boy. I cannot think about it without breaking up. Oh, God, that it had never happened!

I heard the sharp retort of a gun firing when I pulled into the garage. It took me no longer than a minute to race through the house and find her blood-splattered body lying in the position she had twisted herself into after the rifle fired. She had already ceased breathing.

So much of it is a blur after that. Carmelita came in from the grocery store with a load of purchases about the time a shrieking ambulance drove up.

She went all to pieces. "But she was asleep when I left. Never should I have gone out, Hank. Oh, Señor, it es all my fault that she es dead."

"Did you go out the front door?"

"No Señor, it was closed. It had not been opened since yesterday, I think."

The police were very thorough in their investigation. "Was it your gun?"

"Yes, I carried it in my gun rack in my pickup."

"Was it there the last time you used your vehicle?"

"It could not have been. It was still dark when I left this morning."

"Where have you been?"

"Granbury to the lake," I answered.

"Can you prove it?"

"I was with a friend."

"His name?"

"Her. Mary."

"How long have you known this woman?"

"Two years."

"Intimately?"

"Not since Peggy and I married."

Then they read me my rights. I chose to remain silent. They took me to the police station and booked me before they locked me up.

The jailer gave me a newspaper shortly afterwards. The headlines screamed: "PROMINENT BAPTIST MINISTER ACCUSED OF KILLING WIFE WITH BOOBY TRAP. One of Fort Worth's most well-known preachers, President of the Southern Baptist Convention, rodeo rider, spends morning at lake with lover and shoots pregnant wife in afternoon."

There was a mob at the jail door screaming that I be lynched. One man kept screaming over and over, "He killed his own baby."

Mother was there the next morning. "Hank, we are standing by you. You have plenty of money for the best lawyer. I have to know, did you do it?"

"No, Mother, she must have taken the rifle out after we got back from church. Perhaps she planned this after she saw Mary and me talking at the church last night."

"Hank, that is all I need to know. We will fight."

It was a fight. They stripped me of all my duties in the church and convention even before the trial began. A committee at school even voted not to give me my doctor's degree, which was something I had earned.

Mary came to see me the second day. "You should not have

come, Mary," I said through the bars that separated us.

"Hank, I had to give my statement to your lawyer. They will have me on the witness stand. I specifically noticed that your rifle was not in its customary place when we rode to the lake."

"Now they are saying I fixed the rifle before going to the lake," I told her.

"The Postman would have seen it."

"We get our mail at the Post Office."

"Wouldn't someone have seen it from the street?"

"No. Our house is set back almost a half block with large cedar trees down the walk. No one could have seen."

"Milk man?" Mary kept asking.

"We buy our milk at the store."

"I am standing by you, Hank. When this is over, you are marrying me."

There were tears in my eyes when she had to leave.

Next morning's paper had Mary's picture on half of the front page. They accused her of committing adultery just before Peggy's shooting.

The Fort Worth Star Telegram screamed headlines for two months. It was the story that got them the Pulitzer Prize that year.

When they started the trial, there was one particularly seedy-looking man there at every session. He looked to be a street person. I commented on it to my lawyer.

"We will check him out. Some of them come to court to have a place to sit. Mostly they are here in winter."

My act played to a full house each day. Mary testified. They gave her police protection.

It was spring now. I could see daffodils blooming when they took me to court each morning in chains, accompanied by two burly policemen. The memory of those chains will never go away!

What interested me most was the diagrams showing how the gun was fixed to fire. Someone took a strong cord and tied it around the trigger in a slip noose so when she pulled the door sharply open it would cause enough pressure on the gun to fire it. She must have been planning that for weeks.

Mary's testimony established nothing except that I was not home part of the day Peggy was shot. The state's prosecutor used her to verify that the two of us had a long standing sexual relationship. The crowded courtroom was tense when testimony brought out how my invalid wife, Sadie, was duped.

Throughout the trial, I kept catching the eye of that street person. It was as though his large brown eyes were trying to communicate something to me. As the state's prosecuting attorney made point after point, he looked at me. Was he, a street person, envious of me, who had so much, and he so little?

More than twenty witnesses testified about Mary and me. The prosecutor also revealed that I had been arrested as a teenager for drinking.

Even though my staunchest friends testified of my integrity and outstanding work in religion, they could not erase the irrevocable damage. All that had gone on before was a distant blur through which Peggy's death came so vividly. All my achievements as author, preacher, councilor and friend went up in smoke in those few days in Tarrant County courthouse.

The jury was out less than an hour. Apparently, nothing my lawyer told them about the case influenced them. All they could listen to was my affair with Mary.

Mary sat with Mother every day. Neither of them ever left the courtroom until the long trial was over.

"All stand. What is the decision of the Jury?" the judge asked.

"Guilty, your Honor. First degree, premeditated murder."

"Death in the electric chair," the judge started to bang his gavel and dismiss the court.

"Pardon me, your Honor," the words rang out. All eyes turned on the tramp.

"What is it? This has been a hard and tiring trial. You had better have something worthwhile to say."

"Your Honor, this man is innocent."

"How do you know?"

"On the day of the shooting, I slept curled up under shrubbery by the accused's home."

"Will you come before this court and tell these people what you saw?"

My lawyer was on his feet immediately. "Your Honor, I request permission to cross-examine this witness."

"Permission granted."

"Your Honor," the prosecuting attorney protested. "I must have time to prepare a case against what this man has to say."

"Overruled."

"Your Honor, I have sat here day after day and held my mouth. The deceased came out and fixed the murder weapon in position herself on the day of her death."

"Why have you waited until today to come forward with this information?" my lawyer asked.

"When you find out who I am, you will understand. I am on probation from Huntsville, where the state held me for twelve years for a crime I did not commit. Any charge of vagrancy could put me back."

"Why were you in this yard at this particular time?"

"It was a cool night. With some newspapers and an old blanket, I was able to fix a shelter in among the shrubs."

"Tell us what you saw," my lawyer said.

"The young lady got out of her car that morning, slammed the door and angrily brought a rifle around to the front of her house. She was obviously very pregnant. She tied the rifle to the porch railing using a piece of clothesline wire. It took her a half hour. When the defendant drove up in his pickup, she disappeared inside. There was a loud retort and the rifle was left smoking on the porch. It was a short time later when this man, whom, you have falsely accused, came out and hastily examined the fired rifle."

"How can we prove the accused did not pay you to tell this story?" the judge asked.

"I can identify the policeman who picked up the ejected bullet. He is seated over there by the accused."

"Another cheap trick," the prosecutor screamed, "This is a cheap publicity stunt to get a guilty man set free."

I watched the tramp as his face worked under the burden of

thinking. His sorrowful eyes met mine. There was a faint glimmer of hope in his eyes. "Your Honor, I can tell of a thing the policeman did that will prove my story is true."

"Speak up man, a man's life is at stake here."

"This policeman relieved himself in the bushes."

"Is that true?" the judge asked.

Flustered, with a red face, the policeman said, "There was no one around. Yes, I did."

There was pandemonium in the courtroom. Reporters ran to phone their story.

It was a week before they released me, a week during which a glimmer of hope stole through the steel bars where daylight never showed. My lawyer kept in constant touch. They had given the tramp a lie detector test. There was no doubt my savior was telling the truth. I was a free man.

When I walked out the courthouse door, Mary held her arms out to me, and, while cameras flashed, she kissed me hard on my lips.

"Hank, I lost you twice. Once almost for good. You are coming home with me this time. Your mother has been staying with me until this is over."

We drove out into a strange world with flowers blooming and leaves on the trees. They were barely budding when I was locked up.

One of my lives had closed. When Mary stopped and we embraced, new life opened. I was free. This new life did not include the title "Preacher."

CHAPTER
NINETEEN

Fame is like flames fleeing across the prairie, consuming grass as they go. So went my days of glory, like sand pouring too quickly through an hourglass. They stripped all my honors from me, even after the street person's testimony proved I was not guilty of the heinous crime of killing my wife and unborn child.

This is almost my second year back in Mew Mexico. Once again new life breaks out, as grass greens and springs up, renewed by winter snow. For a season it will be green and luxuriant, but soon summer's hot sun will once again cause it to wither and die away, even as my life had flourished and died.

My mother and Sadie's parents are still alive. We see each other daily, even though I live in my new home half way between. At times there is deep contentment in being with those who stood by my side when the going was rough.

Sadie's father said one morning when we were saddling up, "Hank, it is the best thing ever happened for all of us. My age has crept up on me. 'Bout to have to sell out and go to town and live. You might not make as much out here taking care of these cows, but you will find a lot more contentment."

"At least they do not carry a lot of fool ideas of what is right and wrong. Thought I could change people's thinking. All the work I did is gone like it never existed. There is a big engraving over the front entrance to one of our seminaries which, translated from the Greek, reads, `AND THE TRUTH SHALL MAKE YOU FREE.' It is not that way at all. Truth is bondage for people who know it. Only time truth makes people free is when they find something everyone else agrees with," I said half to myself but loud enough for the one I loved like my own father to hear.

"Hank, trouble with you and Sadie, you saw things differently than other people. Take that paper you published on Baptists changing `P's' to `B's'. How many common old Baptist church members will go to the trouble of going to a research library and looking through a bunch of old books to find out if you are right?" Sadie's father could think more clearly than me.

"Man who has the loudest voice in an argument usually wins the fight. You tried to tell people there was room for human error even in the Bible, but how many people can read Hebrew and Greek to check up on your stories? Now, I believe you when you say some of the Bible might have gotten in by a scribe writing something in the margins of a manuscript about being sleepy, but there's no way I can prove it. All those people you were fighting were just waiting for you to stub your toe so they could jump all over you like a bunch of maggots on rotten meat. Reckon you will ever go back to preaching?"

"No, my credibility is broken. No one would listen. Take Mary. She is the best woman on earth since Sadie's dead. Do you think people would want her for a preacher's wife? All they would do is call her an adulteress. I would not put her through it."

For a time after it happened, and before I married Mary, it depressed me awfully. I still had a lot of bitterness. It was an acid in my insides that gnawed at me like a rat gnawing at a board. It was coming down and turning my mind into whey.

You will not know until it happens to you, being given so many responsibilities of seeing after so many things and having it all stripped away. Some of it was my fault, like going to see Mary that day. She was a friend; we did not do anything wrong, we only shared a little affection.

Why does a person have to quit living because he or she get married? Mary and I shared times that we could not erase just because Peggy and I said, "I do." If we were running 'round together all the time, it would have been wrong, but taking her for a ride in a motorboat was not wrong, nor was sharing a few tender minutes together. Most people did not agree with me. There was enough mail blaming me for what happened for me to know how people felt.

Mother talked to me pretty stern, "Hank, you are going to have to snap out of it. You cannot go on living like you are doing. You will dry up and turn into a bitterweed not even fit for the cows to eat. Why don't you drive down to Texas and find Mary? Tell her you are ready to marry her and bring her back here."

"She will not marry me."

"Not what she tells me in her letters. She is waiting for you to come to your senses. Know it is awful hard on you losing two wives so sudden. Sadie was a good woman, but Peggy was a rotten, spoiled child who would never grow up. Someday you will come to your senses and realize it."

"She was carrying my son."

"Killed him, too."

Try as they might, they were unable to cause me to lose my depression. I was in the saddle from daylight to dark that first summer. We let most of the hands go, and I took care of things with Sadie's dad's help. We rode fences, checked on cows and lay under the shade of mesquites and willows in the heat of the day.

It was these sessions, him lying there with his hat over his face and me sitting up fidgeting with restlessness that finally started to bring me out of it, that and the storm.

We got one of those flash floods down a draw west of the house. With that much land to take care of, the weather was never the same anywhere else on the place. I would pull out at daybreak to ride fence that needed some repair.

There was a rocky gorge coming down through this land that a horse could not cross. My horse and I jousted around in the pickup and horse trailer for half a day before we got to the stopping place.

When I let the horse out of the pickup, he came out of the trailer right onto a coyote and almost ran away. His eyes got real wide and showed his whites when he pulled at his reins with me holding on tight. All I needed was to chase a loose horse out here, with the next cross fence ten miles back.

It was a hot, sultry day, with thunderclouds building up back in the northwest. New Mexico has a lot more of those thunderclouds than it has any rain come out of them. The only thing was, after I got on my horse and had a chance to calm him down, there was a lightning streak across the sky. It was too far away for the sound of thunder to reach me. There was not even a cool breeze blowing down across the heat.

The way that cloud looked should have changed my mind about riding across that deep arroyo and off into rough, back country by myself.

Pretty soon, fixing broken wire took all my attention. It was new wire, but fencing crews had stretched it too tight and it was breaking every mile or two. All I did was take extra wire and splice in here and there. It was nothing to hurry about. In fact, I figured on taking at least a week to fix things.

Sunshine on a hot day will do more to make a man forget bad things than anything else. It is like each droplet of sweat lets out a little poison. It was not as though preaching was my soul and life, like some of those people in seminary, who thought God could not run the Baptist church without their being there. Since it had been an accident that preaching took me over, there was not any reason why I could not walk out and leave it the same way I took it up.

There were times it seemed like Sadie was right there with me, trying to help me work out things. Did you ever wonder if dead people come back to help their loved ones? I will tell you one thing for sure, Peggy never did come back and help me out except to give me some awful nightmares.

I had pulled across two or three draws, both dry, when, glancing back to the northwest, I saw that the dark cloud was almost on me. Putting my spurs to my frightened horse, we raced across the bald prairie trying to reach some kind of shelter.

Ahead of me was a dropping off place, down into an area full of cliffs and buttes that could give us protection.

It was not my fate to reach safety. As though all the fury of the gods came down upon me, streaks of lightning cut across the summer sky. Jagged light and then roars of thunder, it was as though this summer storm vented its fury upon the dry ground, trying to wipe me off the face of the earth. My horse stumbled, pitching me to the ground.

A streak of lightning struck my horse and somehow, miraculously, missed me. There was a smell of brimstone in the air when the animal breathed its last breath.

The pelting hail fell before the summer storm. Grass and desert shrubs felt the onslaught of nature's fury. Green leaves shredded into ribbons.

Quickly, I unsheathed my knife and cut the cinch. Placing the saddle over my head, I hunched down under the dead horse's neck. Jagged pieces of ice fell from the storm, until my legs were a lacerated mess.

After the hail ceased, there was a torrential downpour. It swept across me. Rain pelted the vegetation until there was only a solid world of dark, falling water.

It was night before it was safe to come out from under my saddle and start my silent journey through this sodden world, where rain fell occasionally throughout the night. It would stop and then start again sometimes with a fury that threatened to wash away my drenched clothing.

It was no use to pack my saddle. All I could do was mount it on a strand of wire and let it wait for my return. That time, the night and the two days I lived out there, was the beginning of my recovery from the furies that dwelt in my head.

Water sloshed in my rawhide boots; my Levis pressed against my body like a shrunken glove. Like a wild animal, I sought shelter where I could find it.

Water marooned me from my pickup and home, until, under a beating sun, the waters receded. I could safely cross the rain-swollen stream by swimming frantically against the rolling, mud-thickened water.

Once in mid-stream, a desire came over me to let go and let the angry waters tear me on down stream. At last, nothing would be left of me but a swollen body, water-logged with mud and debris. It was only when this suicidal thought struck me that once again my feet and hands reached out to swim across the torrent.

The drenching cleansed me of both Sadie and Peggy, and I

entered a new world. A baptism of fire and water cleansed me.

Mary was waiting for me where I had left her. At first she could not believe her eyes when I drove in her long driveway. It was only when I was halfway to the front door that she came flying out. Talk about a man being calf roped, she lit into me so hard it was all I could do to stand up.

She was all over me with her arms and hands. We kissed until we had to come up for air. I had wondered if she still wanted me. But I had no doubt about it now.

We did not talk much once we got inside the house. The only things we said for a long time were things like, "That feels so good," or "Do it again."

On the second day, we went into Granbury and got married by a Justice of the Peace. Even as secret as we were, a newspaper man got word of it and almost tore us up. It made big headlines all over the state. They rehashed the whole rotten mess. They really had a field day over the fact we had only waited three months after the trial to marry.

Peggy's daddy made a big to-do of disinheriting me legally, but I never had an eye on her fortune. It did not belong to me. It will be interesting to see what happens to his millions with no other close relatives on either his or his wife's side. Probably some Baptist school will build a new hall of learning and name it after him. That would be best.

He did write me a letter and ask how on earth I could remarry so soon after his daughter's death. "Hank," he wrote, "how you could marry that woman who caused my daughter's death is beyond me. She is a common harlot if you ask me. Christians should take her out and stone her after ruining my poor daughter's life like she did. Sometimes I feel like taking a pistol to both of you."

I sent him a New Testament with passages like "Judge not, lest you be judged," underlined in red ink. We will probably never write each other again. It is understandable that he is so bitter, but I did not kill her, nor did I want her dead. Had she given me time, we might have worked out a decent marriage, especially since I wanted our boy so bad. That is what has hurt me the most, the death of my son.

CHAPTER
TWENTY

Mary followed me like she did when we first met on the now almost forgotten Gulf Coast. There was a mellowness that descended on my world. With the first coolness of approaching fall, we settled into a routine of working together.

We built and repaired fence. She was as good on a horse as any Nara Visa cowboy. She mounted a palomino, and I once again rode a coal black horse, a younger brother of the one killed by lightning.

There was a closeness between us that was even closer than the bond between Sadie and me. Mary accepted my mother and Sadie's parents like they were her own. We lived with Mother while carpenters built our house.

Never in the time we shared living quarters did we ever have cross words with one another. It seemed like Mary was the long-lost daughter Mother had searched for all these years.

A happiness came over me that was different from any that I had known before. "Hank, you look like you found heaven," Mother said. "It is so good to have you and Mary here with me."

"It must be an imposition having us stay with you," I said.

"Best time since before your father died. Only thing, is both of you are gone too much," Mother complained.

Mary and I brought our mobile home with us from Texas. When we caught up on work, we traveled across the plains to New Mexico's mountains.

Driving west on Highway 66, we pulled off east of the Sandia Mountains before we reached Albuquerque. After winding up through a steep, treacherous canyon, we came out on the rim of the mountain.

Standing on the sheer drop-off overlooking the Rio Grande Valley, we stood above a cloud cover that prevented us from seeing down below.

"Hank, it is like being in heaven here above the clouds with the sun shining on us."

We were standing close together with my arm around her. It was another world through which we traveled. Aspen trees were beginning to turn a golden-yellow. They quivered in a constant nervous twisting and turning.

Next day, after the clouds dispersed, we were able to see the sun-drenched valley that is Albuquerque and the silver ribbon of the Rio Grande that dissects it. Mary started helping me replace my shattered faith. "Hank, even if God is punishing you, He will not do it forever. Can't you see that if Peggy had not killed herself over the two of us, she would have killed herself for some other reason?" she asked softly.

"You studied enough psychology to know people who are potential suicides will go off the deep end over anything. She would have found something else with which she could not cope before she brought the gun or a knife to her bosom. Just be thankful she did not take you with her."

"Except for you, Mary, it would have been a relief for me to die."

"Do not ever say that, Hank. Life's too precious for a person to spill it himself." It was then she completely surprised me. "Hank, I think I am going to have your child."

"You said there was not a possibility."

"Sometimes doctors are wrong about these things."

A sense of pride came over me when I thought about a new life brought on this earth by my power. It was as though I was a god, with power within me to reproduce.

When I slipped my hand into her blouse and felt with my fingers, a new life surged up within me. Blood pounded in my loins when Mary and I explored where life was starting once again from my seed. This time there would a new life.

"Hank," Mary said one fall morning, "you are like a mother hen.

It is not going to hurt me to ride horseback for a few more months. Nor is it going to hurt for me to help around here."

"Your doctor told you that?"

"Yes, silly. A baby's about the most protected thing there is. God seals it in a cocoon. I am going to protect myself and your son like it was you."

"You are sure it is a boy?"

"Just by old wives' tales, Hank, about how I am carrying him and how he kicks."

Unlike Peggy, Mary did not draw away from me when I played with my developing child. In fact, both of us started loving this third member of our family together. "Hank, I sometimes wonder if babies know when they are in the womb, whether parents want them or not."

"Ours should know it is wanted the way we make over it."

"You know," Mary continued, "there may be a hormone produced by a happy mother that does affect the fetus."

I said, "Imagine heredity has a lot to do with it, don't you? Circumstances play a part. Think, if that tramp had not been sleeping in that hedge, I would be in Huntsville, awaiting the electric chair. Think about how one little thing can make or keep a man from being a criminal. You and me practically living together while Sadie was alive was not breaking society's legal laws, but when the law connected it with Peggy's death, it almost got me killed."

"I think I see what you are driving at, Hank. You mean First Baptist Church in Bulton would not have approved of you and me doing what we did if they knew, but a policeman would not put us in jail for what we did."

"Not unless he caught us naked on the beach."

Mary's face reddened. "Hank, I love you."

I took her in my arms and kissed her tenderly. Our child kicked at being disturbed. "But Mary, when the prosecuting attorney brought our affair up in court, it lowered me in society's eyes. This, plus circumstantial evidence, drove the jury's minds against me."

"Hank, if you had known our being together was going to turn out the way it did, would you have still done what you did?"

"Of course."

"Why? You have paid a terrible price." It was as though she was at last coming to me for approval. I had to handle this carefully.

Looking her in the eyes, I said, "But I have received a wonderful reward, Mary."

She burst out crying against my chest. "Hank, why did you answer that way?"

"Honey, because you are the only woman who ever satisfied me. It does not matter if we are lying on the ground or in a bed, your love makes me a whole person."

She cried until I made tender love to her.

It seems odd that it was not a church member from either church in Texas who came by to see me, but my friend the English teacher. His eyes twinkled and his face lit up when he walked across the pasture in his tweed clothes and his jaunty cap to greet me.

"Hank, you are hiding your talents here."

"Professor, I am glad prison officials did not fry my talents down at Huntsville. Way things were going, my chances of staying alive were not worth a Chinaman's chance."

"Looked like you were guilty as everything there for awhile. Accident you came out of it. Guess it was not as hard on you knowing you were not guilty," the professor said.

"I would have been as dead not guilty as I would have been guilty."

"Wonder how many innocent people are put to death?"

"Might be more than we know. Reason I oppose the death sentence so much. Of course, it keeps some people from committing murder, but there is always that one chance a man is not guilty."

"The only person I could put to death is one caught by an eyewitness committing a murder," he said.

"Guess you are right, but there is still a possibility that even an eyewitness might lie. What brings you up here?" I asked.

"Seminar at Canyon. It is close enough that I wanted to talk to you."

"Glad you did."

"You know, you are the only one who ever made me wonder if

there could not be something to religion. It always seemed like hogwash to me."

"Then you have joined the church?"

"Not hardly," he gave a dry chuckle, "but I am nicer to religious workers who come into my classes. Used to be when one stuck his nose in the door, it would make my blood boil. Now I think of you and I am a little more tolerant."

"Why me? It looks like I confirmed that preachers are a no 'count bunch, who do not deserve a kick in the ass."

"You are one of the only ones who does deserve consideration. You face problems and admit other people exist even though they do not believe like you do."

"That is a compliment coming from you, Professor."

Mary came out and I introduced her to my friend. She drew close to me as if for protection. "You are the first person from Texas to come to see Hank. You are a much better Christian than some of those Bible thumpers."

"Oh please, Mary, do not put me in that category. I deserve better than that." His face broke into a radiant beam when he looked her straight in the eyes. "Looks like Hank finally found what he was looking for."

"Sure have. It will not be long until I will have two," I said with pride.

"Noticed that."

"Come on in and eat with us, Professor," Mary invited. She knew it would please me.

"Sure it will not be too much trouble?" he asked.

"Seems odd, but Mother and I added enough steaks to feed you well."

"Looks like I am in luck. Nice looking house going up," he said.

"It is ours. Hank's building it for us. Even has a nursery."

"You will need it." He gave a dry chuckle that made his eyes crinkle.

"And want it," I said.

After lunch, the Professor and I sat out on the front porch in the coolness of fall. "You have any plans, Hank?"

"Run these two places," I answered.

"I mean with your theological training."

"Guess that is a dead duck with no way of reviving."

"Why?" he asked.

"One error is all the Baptists gives a man."

"Seems like to me you are living more to your convictions now, one woman and all."

"Does not make any difference to my church. They will let me be a member, but they do not want me in their work. Besides Mary won't consent to a religious job."

He said, "Maybe you have not presented her with the right one. Seems like such a waste with all your training going down the drain. Your study on conversion is going to be a classic right along with James's Varieties of Religious Experience. Only thing is, your work is more important. Ever figure out how to predict the results of a religious experience?"

"Hadn't thought about it much. Problem is, there are so many factors: a person's life, early childhood, schooling, work, guilts, satisfactions of sex and religion. All this is brought together by a religious experience that adds another factor. Could these new computers help figure out the results? Of course, you do not believe in the validity of Christian conversion experience."

"Of course I do, Hank. I have seen it happen. Some of those college students' lives turned completely around. I have also seen similar things happen in some of my literature courses. A student comes in mad at the world. He reads something that makes him think. Right before your eyes, a new experience. Results are not as spectacular, but you do not have the danger of developing a religious fanatic."

"How about some of these hippies running around shouting all these political slogans and blowing their minds with pot or liquor?"

"Hank, you are the only preacher who ever made me think. Some of them do blow their minds, don't they?"

"Professor, I did not mean to argue with you. If it were only possible to take a new part, so to speak, and stick it in the human mind. Think about how many millions of dollars are going up in smoke in prisons and mental hospitals alone. Somehow there ought to be a way to repair human minds like they repair cars."

"It is an interesting concept. Religion can do it in some cases. Education can do it in other cases. Neither process works often enough to change the people in large numbers." He crinkled his eyes again when he finished speaking.

"Thanks for getting me to thinking about it," I said.

"You receive your Doctorate?" he asked.

"Doubtful if I ever will."

"Did the work, didn't you?"

"Does not matter. They can hold it up on moral grounds."

"You go to church?"

"Even teach Sunday School. Both Mary and me."

"Seems you should work into something a little more meaningful." He was careful to not make me angry by prying.

The Professor was the first of those who came. Next, Seminary officials presented my diploma in absentia. My real honor came when two Navahos from Shiprock, over in the northwestern corner of New Mexico, showed up looking for work.

Tom White Eagle and Irie Tract drove up in a broken-down Ford touring car, 1950 vintage. They swaggered up to the house and knocked on the door.

"Help you?" I asked.

"We need jobs."

We introduced ourselves. Tom was about thirty, pot-bellied with liquor on his breath. Irie was about the same age, but he was slender.

"Can you build fences?"

"Built a few in our lives and tore down some more," Tom said.

"Tore them down?"

"Vietnam," Irie explained in one angry spat out word.

"Both of you?"

"Both of us," Tom answered.

"I have a tent. You have any sleeping and cooking equipment?"

They ran their old car down along the barbwire fence looking for breaks. Their car shimmied and shook as it bounced along over

185

rough clumps of grama grass. Smoke poured out the tail pipe in a blue cloud, polluting New Mexico's clear, blue air with a haze that dipped and swirled with the autumn breeze.

Tom and Irie were to become my ticket out of a one-way hell of doubt and mistrust. My self-esteem had been shattered so badly that all I could think about was that the whole south knew about my guilt.

Mary came up behind me one morning while I was busy unraveling a ball of twine. Running her hands in my Levi pockets, she started loving me. "Hank, I have been thinking."

"Woman, what you are doing to me, I know what you've been thinking."

"Not only that. You have gone off the deep end in your guilt trip. You've tried to save Bulton and Fort Worth. Maybe there is some lesser kingdom you can conquer."

"Like what?"

"Look around you, Hank."

"Only thing around here that needs converting are two Indians who work their tails off and then get drunker than skunks."

"Those two are going to kill all of us if we do not do something about them quick. How do they make those cars backfire at two o'clock in the morning like they do?"

"I did not hear them, but the way you are going, you are going to get something here in a minute, Mary."

When I turned around to press my body against her, she said, "They had better get that thing fixed before our son gets here. They better not wake him up early." She did not have a chance to finish.

Tom and Irie were my textbooks for studying racial minorities. Only thing, they studied me more than I studied them. Dressed in Levis and flannel shirts, they wore their long, black hair almost to their shoulders. What made it doubly ludicrous was that on their heads, they wore the black, uncreased hats of the traditional Navaho.

On really cold mornings they wore their beat up Army fatigue shirts with corporal's stripes on them. Tom wore a Silver Star above his heart. Irie wore a Congressional Medal of Honor. Out here digging fence post and later helping me put out range cubes, they wore their battle ribbons from Vietnam.

We got used to riding 'round in the pickup cab together, me driving and the two warriors riding with their arms thrown around each other. It got to where Sadie's dad laughed at us. "Hank, you three are quite a group riding in that pickup cab together, those Indians and you. If you would let your hair grow out and get you a Navaho hat, no one could tell you apart." We laughed about it together. A comradeship had grown up between us. He treated Mary like a daughter. "Hank, you are letting Mary do too much with her carrying that baby."

"Mary has a mind of her own just like Sadie did. She has promised to stop riding horseback until the baby's born."

"We want that baby around here. Hank, it has to be so someone can take over running this ranch after you leave."

"Not expecting me to leave anytime soon, are you?"

"You will, Hank. You are educated. People will overlook and forgive you one of these days. You will find something to do that will take you away from here."

"Only job I will take would be one that will let me run this place. Maybe a traveling kind of thing, Dad."

"I'm glad you are thinking about it, Hank. Don't you ever take Mary and that boy away from here like you did my daughter."

"Going to be a big disappointment if that boy turns out to be a girl."

Tom and Irie came up in their old car, and I piled in with them to get horses to look for cows. While we rode, with our breaths making a smoky fog before our faces, Irie and I got to talking about his people. "Bunch of you Navahos, aren't there?" I asked.

"About 90,000 of us stuck out on that land all over New Mexico, Arizona and Utah. Damn government gave us the asshole of the world and expected us to make a living on it."

"Seems like you people have done all right."

"What do you mean, white man who speaks with forked tongue?"

"Increased from 12,000 to 90,000 in less than a hundred years."

"Only thing it proves is we know how to make papoose. Guess you know what a papoose is?"

"No, what?" I asked.

"Chance taken on an Indian blanket." All three of us laughed.

"Any chance of you people doing much better?" I asked.

"If we can keep on selling gas and oil with a little uranium thrown in, we might have you whites working for us instead of us working for you."

"How about cultural changes, Irie?"

"You mean, will we accept your white man God, Hank?"

"Something like that, along with Western civilization's concepts of right and wrong."

"Nothing wrong with our concepts of right and wrong. Only behavioral modification whites have done is keep us from murdering a few of you every year for your scalps."

"Irie," Tom said, "it has been more than that. Look at our cars and pickups. We have white man's refrigerators and stoves. A lot of our people have stopped living in hogans and moved into shack houses thrown up out of rough pine lumber."

"Seen some of those changes," I said. "Dad used to drive me across there when you people were driving big buckboard wagons with yellow wheels. See a buck Indian sitting on the driver's seat and all his women folk and children sitting flat on the wagon bed."

"We know how to keep our squaws in place. Now we sit in the pickup cab and put our squaws and children flat on the pickup bed in back." Tom laughed at this tribal custom.

"Wonder you do not freeze a few," I said.

"Indians are tough."

"Guess you would not have survived without being tough."

Irie said, "That is right. Only thing, we cannot compete in a white man's world. Too many of us are having to leave the reservation and take jobs like Tom and I."

My knowledge of Hebrew and Greek, plus German and a smattering of Spanish, paid off. Tom and Irie sat out to teach me Navaho, that strange language of inflections and chanting, where one rise in tone can cause a person to say something not meant.

We worked together, with them teaching me. Sometimes they laughed and called me a forked tongue white man, but I learned the language along with their tribal customs and folklore - as much as they wanted to teach me. They taught me that Navaho clans had mama at the head - same as in white families, but they admitted it.

"A long time ago," Irie, the quiet one told me, "Indians came to this world from down under on a ship which turned to rock. That is why we have Shiprock."

Anyone who has traveled across Navaho-land will remember seeing this gigantic rock that looms up against the sky in northwestern New Mexico. It is an enormous, spectacular remnant of an ancient geological phenomenon. Like so many of the earth's odd formations, the Ancients gave it religious significance.

"Irie, do you believe that giant rock is really the ship on which your people came into this world?"

"Hank, do you really believe that story about the catfish head and crucifixion, or that Santa Claus really comes down chimneys?"

"Guess if people ever come here from a culture different from ours, we will have a lot of explaining to do," I answered thoughtfully.

"Same way with us Navahos. Some of our people believe lore taught us by word of mouth, but some of us enjoy the rich heritage of our culture."

"How much schooling do you two have?" I asked.

"Tom graduated from the University of New Mexico. I only received a Ph.D. from the University of Arizona."

"You are digging postholes?"

Irie said, "Beats rubbin' asses with those white bastards."

"Ever plan on doing anything with your education?"

"If Vietnam ever wears off Tom. They were fixing to put him in Los Lunas mental hospital."

"What did he do?" I asked.

"Peed in the governor's flower garden."

"Can't say I blame them."

"Right on his roses."

"Don't you plan on going back to the Reservation and using all that education to help your people?"

"'Bout the time you go back and use your nine years, white man," Tom growled.

This was one of our longest conversations. Usually, when we worked together, the two of them, who had grown up together out among the cedars and pinyons, grunted or talked rapidly in their native tongue. Gradually, with one or the other helping, they were making sense to me.

The Sheriff drove out from Nara Visa one wintery New Year's Day. It was not snowing, but there was a biting wind blowing straight from the North Pole. He huddled down in his sheepskin coat when he walked across the windswept yard. I watched him hunkering down trying to keep warm. Not even waiting for his knock, I opened the door for him.

"Come on in, Sheriff. Awful cold day to be driving around for pleasure."

He headed for the gas space heater and started rubbing his hands. "Hank, you lose two Navahos?"

"They went into town last night to celebrate. Something wrong?"

"Not exactly right. They had a few beers they sponged off customers. No one in town will sell liquor to an Indian. Then Tom decided to do a war dance."

"Can't see anything wrong with that. Should have been interesting." I did not really want to hear the rest, but neither did I want to throw range cubes all winter by myself, much less pull cows out of bog holes and repair fence in zero weather.

"Interesting part about it was when Irie decided they had to have some feathers to perform properly."

"Feathers are kind of scarce on New Years Eve. Did they find any?"

"They went over to Mrs. Jones's chicken house."

"Any luck?"

"They chose a white leghorn and two of her favorite fighting cocks she keeps around for pets."

"Few feathers out of their tails should not hurt anything."

"They plucked those roosters at two o'clock this morning in downtown Nara Visa."

"Kind of noisy?"

190

"It was not the noise, Hank. After they performed some kind of ritual sacrifice, Tom decided to do his dance in the nude with only a feather or two covering his thing."

I could hear Mary and Mother back in the kitchen snickering while they cleaned up after breakfast. I was not exactly able to keep a straight face. "You have to pull them in?" I asked.

"Me and the highway patrolman."

We still had the same one we had had for twenty years. In fact, he was one who picked me up for being drunk that night in high school. I was still mad about being handcuffed. "They did not scalp him, did they?" I asked half hopefully.

"No, but they did manage to smear those entrails all over his face and my new Stetson. Damn Indians. Pardon the language ladies," he hollered back. They were not even trying to hide their laughter anymore.

"That is all right, Sheriff. We are trying to get you some hot coffee going. Be out in a moment," Mother hollered. "Sounds like you had an exciting night."

"Not near as exciting as when Mr. Jones marched up Main Street in his nightgown and took a shot at Tom after we already handcuffed him."

I was getting concerned now, thinking of all those cows to feed. "Hurt him?"

"No. Missed completely and blasted into that fancy lamp shop with all those fake Tiffanys and porcelain figures." I groaned inwardly. This was no way to start a New Year.

"You are expecting my Navahos to pay for all that?"

"Mr. Jones is in the cell next to theirs until he can raise bond."

"Guess you would not be a little lighter on a Vietnam vet suffering stress syndrome?" I asked hopefully thinking of Tom.

"Right now, if I could put them in the electric chair, I would pull the switch."

"Guess you don't feel like talking any kind of fine?" I asked hopefully.

"Thank you for the coffee," he hollered back at Mother and Mary. "Awful good fruitcake. Would you be willing to sign for them? They have enough money to pay for damages. Seems like both of them saved their war pay."

"Not real willingly, but I do not want to shovel range cubes all winter either. They have been good workers."

"Another condition, they have to put a muffler on that car of theirs." I knew Mary's face lit up with this pleasurable news.

"That is going to kill them. They work constantly on ways to make that thing backfire like that," I said.

"Another thing, we have at least a dozen calls every time they come to town. They are not to come into town unless you are with them. They visit a woman who charges them a little. You can let them go there and to the grocery and clothing stores, but they are not allowed to be around any beer or whiskey."

"Awful good men, Sheriff. When are you going to release them?"

"Long towards the end of week if you will come in and pick them up. All that training you have, Hank, you ought to be able to help them out."

"I am trying."

Mary came in to get the empty dishes. "Sheriff, this is my wife."

"Awful pretty woman you got here, Hank."

"Think so myself."

" 'Bout time you had a good life, Hank. Been through a little yourself, haven't you?"

"Nothing I cannot handle, Sheriff. Thanks for coming out. Would you mind taking their car over to the garage for a new muffler?"

"Odd that you should mention that. I did that first thing this morning."

Tom and Irie came home subdued and repentant. Repentant? I would not have trusted those chicken-pluckers in a room full of steel balls unless they were too big to pick up. Even then they would find some devilment to do with them.

Mary and I worried all the way in when we went to get them.
"Think you can handle them, Hank?"

"These men are too good to let go down the drain. Maybe this is why the Lord let things happen like they did."

"Glad you are getting a proper perspective on things. Guess you do not think He might have given you to me?" She scooted over close and put her hands on me. She was the best woman I had ever known.

"Hank," Sheriff said, "I talked pretty straight to these two. Tom is already under a court order for that incident in Santa Fe. Next time it is an institution for him. You two men start talking to Hank. He had some good training in this kind of thing."

They just looked sheepishly at the floor. Only thing about it, they drove home without backfiring or spinning their wheels on gravel even once.

CHAPTER
TWENTY ONE

Trying to help Tom took my mind off my failure. Knowing it was dangerous to try treating an emotionally disturbed patient, my first step was to find professional medical help for him. The nearest and cheapest place was the Veterans Hospital in Albuquerque.

Irie wanted to take him over the mountain once a month for an extended series of treatments.Both Mary and I vetoed that idea. We drove him in the travel trailer, and while he spent a night in the hospital, the two of us enjoyed ourselves in the big city.

Coming out of Fort Worth's metropolitan atmosphere into Nara Visa's small town setting was a hard adjustment for us. This gave us a change until Mary was unable to travel.

Tom and I talked while we drove. He was an old time reservation Indian. "White men have different concepts of right and wrong than we do, Hank. It is hard to explain, but take killing a deer, we have a ceremony in honor of the dead deer's spirit. Not to do this would break a hunting taboo. Your people think this is a superstitious practice we should discontinue. Things your people think are bad, my people do not feel that way. Me dancing in the street would be acceptable behavior in Indian country. Your people punish me."

"How far did you grow up from other people, Tom?"

"At times, twenty miles. Sometimes we moved closer."

"Must have been hard adjusting to people in the Army. Kind of cooped in, perhaps."

Gradually, he opened up and talked to me. "Hank, they came out on the reservation and took Irie and me into school at Shiprock when we were six years old. They did not ask for our parents' permission; they took us. That is all."

"You get homesick?"

"How would you like for strangers to take you away from your mother and father when you were that young?"

"I would not like it at all."

"Those in charge put Irie and me in a room together. All we did was lie awake and plan how we were going to bust that place. We planned well."

"Couldn't you walk out some night when everyone was asleep?"

"They locked us in like animals. Our parents were not allowed to visit, nor were we allowed to go home. They tried to brainwash us from wanting to be out with our sheep and horses." Tom said.

"Irie and I laugh about that worthless reservation land, but Hank, to us it is some of the most beautiful land on God's earth. You take some of those buttes and canyons, they are more beautiful than all the green grass over east of here. This land here, I can identify with, but it is not home."

Knowing if I pried that he would clam up, it was best for me to keep asking questions gently. "Ever run off from school?"

"Irie and I, we planned it all out. It took us two months, but we finally got away. It was not easy, but we noticed one housemother left the door unlocked while she went after her pet dog. She did this every night before bedtime. After careful planning, both of us left easy and undetected," Tom seemed to have trouble remembering.

"You give a Navaho an hour's head start, no white man can find him, even with bloodhounds. Two of us spent a month roaming over the land. We slept in hollowed-out places. Everything we ate, we snared with traps. They never caught us, nor did we ever find our parents. First snowstorm, we came back to school after we decided maybe there was something in white man's books we needed to learn."

"How about the Army?"

"Maneuvers were fun for both of us. Barracks life was worse than school. We ran off twice and Military Police brought us back. First time we did, it cost us commissions in the white man's Army."

"Guess that hurt."

"Think they used it for an excuse. Never did see many Navahos being anything but grunts. They liked to have worked our legs off in 'Nam. We knew how to move around without getting shot. Funny thing about a Navaho, Hank, they feel scared same as any other person, but they will not run. Tribal leaders would kill them when they got home."

"How did you earn your medal?" By this time, both of us were talking pretty much in Navaho. Tom said he had never seen a white man pick it up like I did. Maybe this was why he opened up to me. Doctors at the hospital said he never said a word during their sessions. All he did was sit and grunt. When they found out he was talking to me, we worked out a deal and let him talk and they listened in.

He told me a story about saving his whole squad. They were worming their way through elephant grass when a bunch of Congs opened up on them. Two of their men were hit bad. Tom took one, and left the other to Irie. They had been under fire for two days, when he and Irie crept out through heavy grass and came in behind those yellow bastards.

They only used knives, but every one of those devils was dead when it was over. Tom and Irie had been given medals, but no promotions. Irie could take it. Tom went off his rocker and told the regimental officer that he was a son of a bitch. They locked him up for a week.

"Hank, finally I learned to keep it inside my skull, but it's nearly driven me crazy. Been a white done something like that, they'd made him a general. Two of us, they wrote it off that we were two dumb Indians who did not know any better."

Then he went clear out of his head. I pulled over to the side of the road and we got out and did some pretty rough jogging while he kept talking. I learned this in a psychology class. You take a man prone to violence, you get him running while he ventilates his feelings, and he will be less likely to do violence to himself and others.

He cursed for a long time. Then he said, "Hank, you are a preacher, I should not be talking this way 'round you."

"Tom, my credentials are not worth a plugged nickel. My only concern is helping you."

Then he tore into it again about this being a white man's world, and there was not any justice in it for an Indian. He fell down on his knees in a sandy draw and sobbed his guts out. There was blood on his hands where he cut his tongue while telling his story. I let him cry.

"After Irie and I got home, our people took us out and whipped us, Hank."

"Whipped you?"

"Whipped us. They said we had foreign devils in us. They took willow limbs and scourged our hides." I let him cry a long time.

We were late getting home that night. About two o'clock Mary said, "Hank, I am going to have our baby."

"How long do you think it will be, Mary?"

"I have been a fool and let it go on too long."

"Let's get in the car and head for town."

"No use. It's way past that point, Hank. Hold me."

"Hold you nothing, I am getting help."

First, Mother came. She had me call our doctor, then she started working on Mary. "Hurry, Hank. She is bleeding bad."

"Seems to me Irie had some medical training in the Army," I told Mother.

"Get him in here, fast!" she said.

They were staying in the bunkhouse during the cold weather. He was already half dressed, footing it through the hoary frost.

"Mary?" he asked.

"Think you can help?"

"Too late for doctor?"

"Yes. She is bleeding bad."

Irie had me start boiling water while he performed some magic with his skills. Before long, there was a long wail, followed by a constant squalling. We had a boy. After that night, Tom said he did not need white doctors playing 'round with his brain any longer.

Our doctor arrived about dawn. His car had slid off the road.

"Looks like you had a professional here. Irie, what are you

doing back here in this place digging postholes, when your people need you so badly on the Reservation?"

"Tom needed me worse."

"Tom does not need you any longer. You get on home."

"What will Tom do?"

I spoke up. "I am making him ranch manager. Stick around until Mary and our son are able to travel, we will drive you home. Tom needs your car."

The doctor decided Mary would be better at home rather than moving her into town. "What name do you want on the birth certificate?"

Mary came awake. "Hank," she muttered sleepily.

"Bring Hank in about the middle of the month so we can make a footprint and give him the rest of his shots."

Sadie's parents were down. If ever a boy had people to wait on him, little Hank did. We had over a dozen pictures of him before he was a day old.

It was six weeks before we felt Mary and little Hank were able to make the trip across the state to Shiprock. It was on the trip to Durango that summer long ago, that I had last driven that lonesome road across mountains and over high country to Aztec. This time we turned over to Farmington and traveled down along the San Juan River to that strange village resting under the shadow of the rock.

They had school children out to welcome Irie. All up and down the drive they stood with flags, Irie's people, wanting to welcome him. "Irie, welcome back to your school," the government superintendent said, while he clasped his hand. "We have been waiting ever since we received your letter. There is so much you can do here with your people. If only Tom had come back."

It was by accident that I preached in the Baptist Church in Shiprock on Sunday. Out in sand hills and rocks, we met in a little white church building. They had spread the word around the night before that the great rodeo rider, Hank from Nara Visa, was going to preach.

Throngs of Navahos began to gather well before sunup to listen. Dressed in their bright shirts, the men gathered in groups to talk.

Under cedar shrubs, Indian women in their colorful costumes met with their children to talk with neighbors they had not seen for maybe a year. It was like Indian day down at Gallup.

We met to sing and then I got up to preach in Navaho. A silence spread over the congregation. I knew these were the people I would travel across New Mexico to help whenever I could. From Bulton to Fort Worth, and now to Shiprock, God had brought me home.

I looked at Mary and little Hank. She was crying tears of joy.

END